A MIRROR
MENDED

TORDOTCOM BOOKS BY ALIX E. HARROW

A Spindle Splintered

A MIRROR MENDED

Alix E. Harrow

TOR
DOT
COM

A TOM DOHERTY ASSOCIATES BOOK
NEW YORK

A MIRROR MENDED

Edited by Jonathan Strahan

Interior illustrations by Michael Rogers

A Tordotcom Book
Published by Tom Doherty Associates
120 Broadway
New York, NY 10271

www.tor.com

Tor® is a registered trademark of Macmillan Publishing Group, LLC.

The Library of Congress Cataloging-in-Publication Data is available upon request.

ISBN 978-1-250-76664-9 (hardcover)
ISBN 978-1-250-76665-6 (ebook)

Our books may be purchased in bulk for promotional, educational, or business use. Please contact the Macmillan Corporate and Premium Sales Department at 1-800-221-7945, extension 5442, or by email at MacmillanSpecialMarkets@macmillan.com.

First Edition: 2022

Printed in the United States of America

0 9 8 7 6 5 4 3 2 1

to everyone who is doing their very best just to live, happily

A MIRROR MENDED

1

I LIKE A good happily ever after as much as the next girl, but after sitting through forty-eight different iterations of the same one—forty-nine, if you count my (former) best friends' wedding—I have to say the shine is wearing off a little.

I mean, don't get me wrong, I worked hard for all forty-nine of those happy endings. I've spent the last five years of my life diving through every iteration of Sleeping Beauty, chasing the echoes of my own shitty narrative through time and space and making it a little less shitty, like a cross between Doctor Who and a good editor. I've rescued princesses from space colonies and castles and caves; I've burned spindles and blessed babies; I've gotten drunk with at least twenty good fairies and made out with every member of the royal family. I've seen my story in the past and the future and the never-was-or-will-be; I've seen it gender-flipped, modern, comedic, childish, whimsical, tragic, terrifying, as allegory and fable; I've seen it played out with talking woodland creatures, in rhyming meter, and more than once, God help me, with choreography.

Sure, sometimes I get a little tired of it. Sometimes I wake up and don't know where or when I am, and feel all the stories blurring into a single, endless cycle of pricked fingers and doomed girls. Sometimes I hesitate on the precipice of the next story, exhausted on some fundamental, molecular level, as if my very atoms are worn thin from fighting the laws of physics so hard. Sometimes I would do anything—anything at all—not to know what happens next.

But I spent the first twenty-one years of my life being Zinnia Gray the Dying Girl, killing time until my story ended. I'm still technically dying (hey, aren't we all), and my home-world life isn't making headlines (I pick up substitute teaching shifts between adventures, and have spent the last couple of summers working the Bristol Ren Faire, where I sell the world's most convincing medieval fashion and ephemera). But I'm also Zinnia Gray the Dimension-Hopping, Damsel-Saving Badass, and I can't quit now. I may not have much of a happily ever after, but I'm going to give away as many as I can before I go.

I just skip the after-parties, that's all. You know—the weddings, the receptions, the balls, the final celebratory scenes before the credits roll. I used to love them, but lately they just feel saccharine, tedious. Like an act of collective denial, because everybody knows that happily is never really *ever after*. The truth is buried in the phrase itself, if you look it up. The original version was "happy in the ever after," which meant something like "hey, everybody dies and goes to heaven in the end, so does it really matter what miseries and disasters befall us on this mortal plane?" Cut out two little words, cover the gap with an -ly, and voilà: The inevitability of death is replaced by the promise of endless, rosy life.

If Charmaine Baldwin (former best friend) heard me talking like that, she'd punch me slightly too hard for it to be a joke and cordially invite me to chill the fuck out. Primrose (former Sleeping Beauty, now part-time ballroom dancing instructor) would fret and wring her pale hands. She might remind me, bracingly, that I'd been granted a miraculous reprieve and ought to count myself lucky! With an audible exclamation point!

Then Charm might casually mention my five years of missed appointments with radiology, the too-many prescriptions I'd left unfilled. At some point the two of them might exchange one of their *looks*, ten thousand megawatts of love so true its passage would leave my eyelashes singed, as if I'd stood too close to a comet.

And I would remember sitting at their wedding reception while they slow danced to that spacey, ironic Lana Del Rey cover of "Once Upon a Dream," looking at each other as if they were the only thing in the only universe that mattered, as if they had forever to look. I would remember getting up and going to the bathroom, meeting my own eyes in the mirror before I pricked my finger on a shard of spindle and vanished.

And hey, before you get the wrong idea, this isn't a love triangle thing. If it were, I could simply say "throuple" three times in the mirror and summon Charm to my bedroom like lesbian Beetlejuice. I'm not jealous of their romance—they love me and I love them, and when they moved to Madison for Charm's internship, they rented a two-bedroom apartment without any discussion at all, even though the rent is ridiculous.

It's just that they're so damn *happy*. I doubt they've ever lain awake at night, feeling the bounds of their narratives like hot wires pressing into their skin, counting each breath and wondering how many are left, wishing—uselessly, stupidly—they'd been born into a better once upon a time.

But that's not how it works. You have to make the best of whatever story you were born into, and if your story happens to suck ass, well, maybe you can do some good before you go.

And if that's not enough, if you still want more in your greedy, selfish heart: I recommend you run, and keep running.

❀ ❀ ❀

ALL THAT SAID, this particular happily ever after is a real banger. It's another wedding reception, but this one has tequila shots and a churro cart, and every single person, including the bride's great-grandmother, is dancing me under the table.

I showed up two weeks ago, following the distant, familiar echo of a young woman cursing her cruel fate. I landed in a palatial bedroom that looked like it was stolen straight from the set of a telenovela and met Rosa, whose one true love had choked on a poison apple and fallen into a coma. The apple threw me, I'll admit, and it took me a while to get the hang of this place—there are more sudden betrayals and identical twins than I'm used to—but eventually I smuggled Rosa past her wicked aunt and into her beloved's hospital room, where-upon she kissed him with such passion that he snapped straight out of his vegetative state and proposed. Rosa stopped kissing him just long enough to say yes.

I tried to bail before the wedding, but Rosa's great-grandmother slapped the spindle out of my hands and reminded me that her wicked aunt was still out there seeking revenge, so I stayed. And, sure enough, the aunt showed up with a last-second plot twist in her back pocket that might have ruined everything. I locked her in the women's room and Rosa's great-grandmother put a ¡CUIDADO! sign out front.

It's after midnight now, but neither the DJ nor the dancers are showing any signs of quitting. Normally I'd have slipped out the back hours ago, but it's hard to feel existential dread when you're full of churros and beer. Plus, the groom's second or third cousin has been shooting me slantwise looks all evening, and everyone in this dimension is so dramatically, excessively hot I've spent half my time blinking and whispering, "Sweet Christ."

So I don't run away. Instead, I look deliberately back at the groom's second or third cousin and take a slow sip of beer. He jerks his chin at the dance floor and I shake my head, not breaking eye contact. His smile belongs on daytime TV.

Ten minutes later, the two of us are fumbling with the key card to his hotel room, laughing, and twenty minutes later I have forgotten about every single dimension except this one.

It's still dark when I wake up. I doubt I've slept for more than two or three hours, but I feel sober and tense, the way I get when I linger too long.

I make myself lie there for a while, admiring the amber slant of the street light across Diego's skin, the gym-sculpted planes of his back. I wonder, briefly, what it would feel like to stay. To wake up every morning in the same world, with the same person. It would be good, I bet. Even great.

But there's a slight tremble in my limbs already, a weight in my lungs like silt settling at the bottom of a river. I don't have time to waste wanting or wishing; it's time to run.

I pick my clothes off the floor and tiptoe to the bathroom, feeling for the handkerchief in my jeans pocket. Wrapped safely inside it is a long, sharp splinter of wood, which I set beside the sink while I dress. I can and have traveled between dimensions with nothing but a bent bobby pin and force of will, but it's easier with a piece of an actual spindle. I'm sure Charm would explain about the psychic weight of repeated motifs and the narrative resonance between worlds if I asked, but I don't ask her anything anymore.

I don't travel as light as I once did, either. These days I carry a shapeless backpack full of basic survival supplies (Clif Bars, bottled water, matches, meds, clean underwear, a cell phone I rarely turn on) and the useful detritus of forty-eight fairy tale worlds (a small sack of gold coins, a compass that points toward wherever I'm trying to go, a tiny mechanical mockingbird that sings shrilly and off-key if I'm in mortal peril).

I sling the pack over my shoulder and glance at the mirror, knowing what I'll see and not really wanting to: a gaunt girl with greasy hair and a too-sharp chin who should definitely text her mom to say she's okay, but who probably won't.

Except, the thing is, it's not me in the mirror.

It's a woman with high, hard cheekbones and hair coiled like a black silk snake on her head. Her lips are a startling false red, painted like a wound across her face, and there are deep pink indents on either side of her brow. She's older than most sleeping beauties—there are cold lines carved at the corners of those red, red lips—and far less pretty. But there's something compelling about her, a gravitational pull I can't explain. Maybe it's the eyes, burning back at me with desperate hunger.

The lips move, silent. *Please.* One hand lifts to the other side of the glass, as if the mirror is a window between us. Her fingertips are a bloodless white.

I've been in the princess-rescuing game long enough that I don't hesitate. I raise my fingers to the glass, too, but there doesn't seem to be anything there. I can feel the heat of her hand, the slight give of her skin.

Then her fingers close like claws around my wrist and pull me through.

* * *

YOU MIGHT THINK interdimensional travel is difficult or frightening, but it's usually not that bad. Picture the multiverse as an endless book with endless pages, where each page is a different reality. If you were to retrace the letters on one of those pages enough times, the paper might grow thin, the ink might bleed through. In this metaphor, I'm the ink, and the ink is totally fine. There's a brief moment when I'm falling from one page to the next, my hair tangling in a wind that smells like old paperbacks and roses, and then someone says *help* and I tumble into another version of my own story.

This time, though, the moment between pages is not brief. It's *vast*. It's a timeless, lightless infinity, like the voids between galaxies. There are no voices calling for help, no glimpses of half-familiar realities. There's nothing at all except the viselike grip of fingers around my wrist and a not-insignificant amount of pain.

I mean, I don't know if I technically "have" a "body," so maybe it's not real pain. Maybe my conviction that my organs are turning themselves inside out is just a really shitty hallucination. Maybe all my neurons are just merely screaming in existential dread. Maybe I'm dying again.

Then there are more pieces of story rushing past me, but I don't recognize any of them: a drop of blood on fresh snow; a heart in a box, wet and raw; a dead girl lying in the woods, pale as bone.

The fingers release my wrist. My knees crash against cold stone. I'm lying flat on my face, feeling like I was recently peeled and salted, regretting every single beer and most of the churros (although nothing I did with Diego).

I attempt to leap to my feet and achieve something closer to a woozy stagger. "It's alright, it's okay." I hold up empty hands to show I mean no harm. The room is spinning unhelpfully. "I'll explain everything, but if there's a spindle in here, please don't touch it."

Someone laughs. It's not a nice laugh.

The room settles to a slow lurch, and I see that it's not a lonely tower room at all. It looks more like the apothecary in a video game—a small room stuffed full of stoppered bottles and glass jars, the shelves loaded with books bound in cracked leather, the counters strewn with silver knives and pestles. If it belongs to a wizard, there are certain indications (a yellowing human skull, chains dangling from the walls) that they are not the friendly kind.

The woman from the mirror is sitting in a high-backed chair beside a fireplace, her chin lifted, gown pooled around her ankles like blood. She's watching me with an expression that doesn't make any sense. I've met forty-nine varieties of Sleeping Beauty by now, and every single one of them—the princesses, the warriors, the witches, the ballet dancers—has looked surprised when a sickly girl in a hoodie and jeans zaps herself into the middle of their story.

This woman does not look surprised. Nor does she look even slightly desperate anymore. She looks *triumphant,* and the sheer intensity of it almost sends me to my knees again.

She studies me, her brows lifted in two disdainful black arches, and her lips curve. It's the kind of smile that doesn't belong on Sleeping Beauty's face: sneering, languorous, strangely seductive. Somewhere deep in my brain, a voice that sounds like Rosa's great-grandmother says, ¡CUIDADO!

She asks sweetly, "Why, what spindle would that be?" which is when I notice three things more or less simultaneously. The first is a small silver mirror in the woman's left hand, which does not seem to be reflecting the room around us. The second is an apple sitting on the counter just behind her. It's the sort of apple a child would draw, glossy and round, poisonously red.

The third is that there is no spinning wheel, or spindle, or shard of flax, or even a sewing needle, anywhere in the room.

Somewhere deep in the bottom of my backpack, muffled by spare clothes and water bottles, comes a tinny, warbling whistle, like a mockingbird singing out of key.

2

SURE, OKAY. I should have figured it out a little faster. But in my defense, my brain was recently soaked in Sol Cerveza, dragged through the liminal space between worlds, and tossed at the feet of a tall woman with silken hair and a dangerous smile.

Also, in five years of adventuring through the multiverse, I've never once made it out of Sleeping Beauty. And let me tell you, I tried. I hung my hair out of high windows and bought apples from old ladies at the farmer's market; I went dancing until the stroke of midnight and asked my father to bring me a single rose from the grocery store. None of it worked. Charm theorized about clusters of related realities and drew graphics that looked like the branches of some great interstellar tree. I pretended like I understood when really all I understood is that there are some rules you can't break.

But now, somehow—my eyes flick to the silver mirror in the woman's hand—the rules have changed. It occurs to me that I have no idea what's going to happen next. A thrill shoots up my spine and buzzes at the back of my skull.

"You," I say, and my voice is shaking now, but not with fear, "are not a princess."

Her perfect brows arch half an inch higher, and I wonder dizzily if this world has eyebrow threading. "Not anymore, no." She touches the pink indent at her left temple, which I'm suddenly sure was left by the weight of a crown.

"So where am I?" But it's a simple equation (apple + mirror + royalty) with only one answer. There are no spindles here, and no fairies, but I'd bet my left lung there are seven dwarves living deep in the woods. "Who are you?"

Her triumph flickers very briefly, as if she doesn't like that question much. "You may call me Your Majesty, or My Queen, should you find yourself begging for mercy."

I've heard more than a few villainous threats, but none delivered with such bored sincerity. My excitement dims somewhat. "Right. Cool. Well, it's an honor." My eyes slide to the only door. I'm several feet closer than she is. "I'm sure you're wondering how I got here—"

Her eyes flash, the triumph swallowed by a bottomless, fascinating hunger that makes me forget, for a moment, that I'm in the middle of an escape attempt. The mockingbird in my bag sings an octave higher. "And I would just love to tell you about it. But, uh, is there a bathroom I could use, first?"

The queen tucks the hunger away with practiced ease, like someone leashing a dog; some very unwise part of me is sorry to see it go. She says with polite amusement, "No, I don't think so."

"Oh." I take a sidling step toward the exit. "Could I at least have something to drink? I have this condition, see, this mysterious illness." Generalized Roseville Malady (GRM) isn't actually that mysterious, but premodern monarchs aren't generally familiar with terms like "amyloidosis" or "in utero genetic damage." "It causes me great suffering, and will one day surely kill me." My only symptoms at the moment are a high heart rate and a headache, which could be explained by being hungover, freaked out, and—sue me—a tiny bit horny, but I drag my hand dramatically across my brow anyway.

The queen looks profoundly unmoved. "How tragic," she says passionlessly. The part of me that isn't busy calculating the distance between me and the exit and the likelihood of dying in a fairy tale I don't even like goes *huh*. Twenty-six years of terminal illness has taught me to anticipate and weaponize pity, however tedious and gross it feels—but the queen's face is the definition of *pitiless*. It would be gratifying if it weren't so inconvenient.

I take another step, edging behind a chair. "It is, truly it is." The queen is watching me in a way that reminds me uncomfortably of a lean-boned stray watching a very stupid robin. "It's a sad tale, which I will relate to you, at length and with footnotes, should you desire it, Your Majesty." On the final syllable I shove the chair hard, sending it tumbling between us, and rush for the door.

I make it, hands slapping hard against the wood, fingers fumbling for the latch—

Which is, as it turns out, locked.

I stand facing the door for a long moment, breathing hard into the silence.

"Oh *dear*," says the queen. "Let me get that for you." I turn to see her carefully righting my tossed chair, setting the mirror on her workbench, and taking a long green ribbon down from a hook. She saunters toward me with a swaying, careless step that makes me think again of a hungry cat, if cats wore crowns and gowns the color of fresh kidneys.

She stops far too close to me, and there might be the teensiest, tiniest delay before I move my eyes from the clean line of her collarbone up to her face. There's a curl in her lip that tells me she noticed.

Her eyes fall to my throat and my brain leaps unhelpfully to that fucked-up Gaiman short story where Snow White is a vampire, and then, even more unhelpfully, to an undergraduate lecture about the inherent homoeroticism of Western vampire literature.

The queen lifts the green ribbon between us. I have time for two very brief and stupid thoughts (*Where's the key?* and *God, that mockingbird is loud*) before her other hand snakes past me and the ribbon is wrapped around my neck.

❋ ❋ ❋

IT DOESN'T SEEM that bad, as garrotings go. The queen barely knots the ribbon before stepping away. But in the startled second it takes my hands to reach my throat, the ribbon has wound itself so tightly that I can't fit my fingers beneath it. It pinches harder, crushing veins, clenching around my windpipe. I try to scream, but nothing emerges except a wet wheeze.

Dark spots bloom across my vision. The back of my head cracks against the door. One of my fingernails snags and rips as I try and fail to tear the ribbon away, and then I'm falling and thinking, with extreme irritation: *I've been here before.* I have been on my knees in some distant Disney-knockoff castle, fighting for air and not finding it. That time there was a princess to kiss me back to life; this time there is a queen to watch me die.

Which is bullshit, because I'm not supposed to die yet. I'm supposed to have years, maybe even decades, and I'll be damned if somebody else's evil stepmother is going to steal them. On this bracing thought, I lunge for the queen's legs. Except it turns out your muscles need oxygen to function, so what I actually do is flop face-first at her feet.

I hear a distant sigh. Hands under my arms, dragging me across the floor. The cold click of metal around my wrists. Just when my vision has contracted to a single point of light and my limbs have gone so numb they feel like bags of wet sand, the ribbon disappears.

There's an ugly little stretch of time here that mostly consists of drooling and choking and the sickly sound of vomit hitting the floor. Let's skip over it.

When I can see again, I find my arms manacled awkwardly above my head, with just enough loose chain to rattle but not enough to either stand or lie down. The queen is carefully emptying my backpack onto the counter, examining each item with mild interest and sorting it according to some ineffable system of her own devising. The socks and underwear are piled together; my phone is held briefly at arm's length, as if she is considering her own reflection in the dark glass of the screen, before being placed carefully beside the knife.

"What," I begin, but I have to stop to wheeze hoarsely between each word. "The *fuck*. Is wrong. With you."

The queen doesn't answer immediately. She's holding my little mechanical mockingbird up to the light; the bird is now producing a pitch only dolphins can hear. "Oh, you're perfectly fine," she assures me without a single atom of remorse. "It would only have sent you into an enchanted slumber."

"*Only*? Jesus Christ, lady, don't they have human rights here? I didn't do anything to you and you just—you—" This time it's a sudden, helpless rage that chokes me. I still dream of my own death sometimes, except now it's a memory instead of a prophecy. I feel my lungs massing with misbegotten proteins, my pulse weakening, my mouth full of air I can no longer breathe. I don't even like holding my breath in the pool anymore or putting my face under the blankets; it turns out I really, really dislike being strangled.

I breathe in through my nose and out through my mouth, just like my stupid therapist taught me, until I can snarl, "Just whack me in the head next time, you fucking psychopath."

"Noted," she replies coolly, still studying the mockingbird. Eventually she sweeps it to the floor and crushes it quite casually beneath her heel. There's a small, pathetic crunch, like several finger bones snapping at once, and the mockingbird is quiet. The silence leaves me chilled, dry-mouthed, unable to believe I permitted myself even a single homoerotic impulse about this woman.

She turns a level, businesslike gaze on me. "Now, let us talk. I require your assistance."

It's hard to pull off a mocking laugh when you're shackled to someone's wall and they're looking at you like you're a lock they will either pick or break, but I give it a good effort. "Really? Because I could swear you just choked me with a magic murder ribbon."

"It's a bodice lace, actually."

"I figured." I may not know this story as well as Sleeping Beauty, but I'm still a folklore major with a significant Grimm obsession. In their version, called either Schneewittchen or Schneeweißchen depending on the edition, the wicked stepmother tries to kill Snow White with a poison comb and a bodice lace before she goes for the apple, which are sufficiently weird murder weapons that my favorite professor even wrote an article about them ("Mirror, Mirror: Vanity as Villainy in the Western Imagination"). If Dr. Bastille were here, she'd probably be asking the queen whether her choice of tools represented a sublimated reclamation of the male monopoly on violence, whereas all I can think about is how badly I want to punch her in the throat. And how I'm going to escape, and whether I have a chance in hell of taking that mirror with me.

The queen watches my sour, snarling mouth for a moment before sighing and dragging her chair to face me. She sits, her kidney-colored gown falling in another perfect sweep around her feet, her face tired beneath the makeup. "Please understand that I will do whatever I must to get what I need." Her eyes are concerningly sincere. "No one will interrupt me. No one will save you." Her accent is lightly burred, her words blunt, nothing like Prim's vaguely British, grammatically suspect speech. I wonder if Charm has finally removed the word *whence* from her vocabulary, and then quickly stop wondering, because thinking about Charm is like thinking about an amputated limb.

"And really," the queen continues. "It is no great favor I ask of you. I only need to know how you do it."

I curl my lip and ask scornfully, "How I do what?" But there's only one thing she could possibly want from me, however unlikely it seems. The hunger has returned to her eyes, and it strikes me, with a sudden, plunging chill, that I've seen it before: staring back at me out of every mirror since I was old enough to understand my own story.

"I want to know how you get out," she grates, and for the first time her voice is something less than perfectly calm. "I want to know how you leave your world and find another."

A heartbeat of silence. Another, while her eyes bore into mine and my brain produces nothing but strings of panicked question marks (????????). I try very hard not to look at her mirror.

"Tell me," she says, imperious, barely leashed, and I feel my chances of getting out of this with all my fingernails and teeth declining precipitously.

I swallow hard and say, "I'm sorry, I don't know what you mean," because I've seen enough Marvel movies to know that it's generally frowned upon to hand the obvious villain the keys to the multiverse. I don't have a clear idea what she'd do with the ability to zap herself into other versions of Snow White, but I doubt it's anything good, and more importantly, fuck her.

The queen's mouth flattens. She holds my very twenty-first century backpack by one fraying strap, her eyebrows raised very slightly.

"Oh, that? I got it from a wizard in a kingdom far from here. I'm happy to draw you a map, if you'd like to talk to him." All I need is about two minutes un-shackled so I can prick my finger and peace the hell out of here, preferably with that magic mirror in tow. I would like to know where it came from, and how the queen found out about multiple worlds in the first place, and why her eyes are so ravenous, so familiar, but it doesn't seem worth lingering to find out.

"I am not," she says gently, "a fool."

"Okay, fine, you got me! I'm from another world. But frankly"—I rattle my chains at her—"I don't see why I should tell you shit."

She rises from her chair, face twisting. The air seems to gather and darken around her like a personal thunderstorm. "Because if you don't, you writhing *maggot*, you miserable *louse*, I will feed your beating heart to the carrion birds. I will knap knives from your bones and use them to flense the fat from your breathing body." She pauses, perhaps to appreciate her own alliteration. "I am the *queen*." There are no sibilants in that sentence, but she manages to hiss it anyway.

My lips peel back from my teeth as I look up at her, not fearless but pissed enough to do a good impression. "Oh, please, you're just the bad guy. The villain, the evil stepmother. You're the Wicked Witch of the East, bro."

She opens her mouth, but I interrupt, entirely unable to resist. "You're going to look at me and you're going to tell me that I'm wrong?

Am I wrong?" At least Charm will be proud of me if these turn out to be my last words.

I watch the queen teetering on some internal precipice, perhaps deciding between the thumbscrews or the pliers. Instead, she tucks her fury carefully away. It's like watching a woman shove a mattress into a pillowcase. She strides to a crowded bookshelf and asks abruptly, "What's your name?"

"Zinnia Gray. Of Ohio."

She takes down a slender volume with a bright red spine, incongruous in the gloom of her workroom. "Aren't you going to ask me my name, Zinnia Gray? Or do they not have manners in Ohio?"

"Whereas here it's customary to chain your visitors to the wall." She studies my face with finite patience, one fingernail tapping the book, until I sigh. "Fine. What's your name?"

Obnoxiously, she doesn't answer. She slinks back over to me and stands, paging through her book. I crane my neck upward, expecting to see a book of hexes or poisons, something with embossed silver and dyed leather, but the cover is simple red canvas, lightly scuffed. It has a tatty ribbon glued to the binding as a bookmark and a purplish stain on the back, and there's something very, very familiar about it. Like, *distressingly* familiar. The kind of familiar that your brain refuses to process because it just doesn't make sense, like seeing your first grade teacher in the grocery store.

I can't read the title upside down and backwards, but I don't have to, because I already know what it says. This book—this *exact copy* of this book, with the tatty ribbon and the grape juice stain on the back cover—has been on my bedside shelf since my sixth birthday. It's the 1995 reprint of *Grimm's Fairy Tales*, with Arthur Rackham's original 1909 illustrations.

This is, I find, my limit. I've been sucked into a story that doesn't belong to me, garroted, chained up, and questioned by a queen, but seeing a fairytale villain with my favorite childhood book is apparently the place where my disbelief draws a hard fucking line in the sand and says: *No way.*

But the book persists in existing, solid red against the white of the queen's fingers, whether or not I believe in it. She finds the page she's looking for and turns the book around, kneeling before me. One page is a full-color plate of a sleeping girl with skin the color of chewed gum and seven small men gathered around her. The other page is dense text with a title in curlicued faux-Victorian font: *Little Snow-White.*

"You were right, of course," the queen says, conversationally. "I *am* the villain, the stepmother, the wicked witch, the evil queen." Her face is racked with furious grief, lips twisting with something far too dark to be humor. She leans past me, so close I can feel the heat of her cheekbone against mine, the slight stirring of my hair as she whispers, "*I don't have a name.*"

3

THE QUEEN DRAWS slowly back from me. She meets my gaze for a long, taut moment, her expression fierce but her eyes full of the impotent ache of someone who knows how their story ends and can't change it. I see, or think I see, the faint sheen of furious tears before she whirls away. The door slams as she leaves and I remember, for the first time in several minutes, to exhale. I suspect I'd feel that way even if the queen hadn't been threatening to rip out my beating heart; she has that kind of presence, an intensity that thickens the air around her.

I knock my head ungently against the wall and order myself to get it together. Luckily, or unluckily, I've been in enough perilous situations by now that I don't waste too much time panicking or regretting my life choices or shouting *SHITSHITSHIT* in all caps. I've developed a simple system.

Step one, which turns out to be equally useful in staving off panic attacks and escaping dungeons, is to make a list of your physical assets. I have a book of fairy tales that shouldn't exist on this narrative plane, a piece of spindle in my back pocket, two bobby pins tucked in my shoe, and a finite number of minutes before the queen returns.

Step two is to make a plan. The obvious choice is to wrangle the splinter out of my jeans, jab my finger, and whisk myself back to the Sleeping Beauty–verse. But I could also go for the bobby pins and try to pick the lock on my shackles (don't laugh—once I realized how often various kings and fairies were going to be tossing me into dungeons and throwing me in the stocks, etc., I spent a serious number of hours watching lock picking YouTube videos. I only have about a 50 percent success rate in the real world, but I've found that fairy tale locks are inclined to pop open at the first sign of narrative agency).

Step three is to get moving. I hesitate for a fraction of a second before going for the pins instead of the splinter. Partly because it would require some pretty uncomfortable contortions to reach my back pocket, whereas all it takes is a half split to grab my ankle, but also because I'm curious. Not about the queen—despite her hungry eyes and her silken hair and the way she looks at me, like I'm something vital, desperately necessary to her survival—but about everything else.

I waggle the bobby pin in the lock while I assemble a list of questions, including but not limited to: How did I pop into Snow White? How did my childhood book wind up in an alternate universe? Did the queen steal it, or did it spontaneously manifest? Is that mirror some kind of palantír/all-knowing orb situation that lets her peek into other worlds? If I steal it, will I be able to escape my story forever? And, PS, has my casual world-hopping had some unfortunate and unforeseen effects on the narrative integrity of the multiverse?

I can't stop myself from picturing the slideshow Charm would assemble for the occasion: *So There's Something Fucky Happening to the Multiverse: Ten Implausible Theories.* Or maybe, *So You're a Little Bit Hot for the Villain: We've All Been There but This Isn't the Time, Babe.*

But Charm stopped answering my texts six months ago, over basically nothing. The last message I have from her is two paragraphs long and calls me "a pretty shitty friend" and "an irresponsible lackwit," among other things. Prim must be rubbing off on her.

Just about the time my wrists are chafed bloody and my tendons are cramping, the manacles pop open. I rub the numbness out of my fingers, shove my stuff back into my pack, and tuck the mirror carefully on top. Its surface is a perfectly mundane reflection, but it feels heavier than mere silver and glass should.

The door isn't locked, which means the queen underestimated me after all. I feel a fleeting, embarrassing twist of disappointment.

I'm three steps into the hall when a heavy hand falls on my shoulder and a cheery voice says, "Pardon, miss."

There's a man standing just outside the workroom door. He has a generic, uncomplicated handsomeness, like one of the lesser Hemsworths, and I'd guess from his callouses and clothes that he's a woodcutter, or—aha!—a huntsman.

I raise my chin to an aristocratic angle. "Unhand me, sir! I am the Lady Zinnia of Ohio, and the queen herself invited me to—"

But he's shaking his head earnestly. "Sorry, miss. Back in you go." He tugs politely at my shoulder as if I'm a pet trying to escape her crate.

"You are mistaken." I keep my voice shrill and disdainful, but my hand is already in my back pocket.

"Her Majesty said if I saw a skinny wastrel in men's trousers I was not to let her escape—"

The huntsman stops because I've driven my fist toward his throat with the long splinter sharp between my knuckles. He catches my wrist in a hand roughly the size and shape of a baseball mitt. He gives my arm a shake that makes my bones creak, and the splinter falls from my nerveless fingers.

He shakes his head again, tsking as he picks up the splinter. "None of that, now. Her Majesty also said I was to whip the flesh from your ribs and leave you hog-tied, awaiting her pleasure, if you gave me any difficulty."

I try to wrench my hand away, but I have the upper body strength of a wet paper doll. I'm not even sure the huntsman notices. "That—okay, that is definitely not necessary." I soften, letting my lashes fall and my lip tremble. "Please, sir, don't hurt me." This seems like a fairly traditional retelling of Snow White, which means the huntsman is a giant softy with a track record of disobeying his queen.

He looks visibly torn, like a good kid thinking about breaking curfew. "Well, let's just get you locked back up, eh? Then she'll be none the wiser." He lays a conspiratorial finger along his nose, which isn't something I thought anyone ever did in real life.

"No, that's not—"

But it's too late. He hauls me back into the queen's work room and snaps the manacles back over my wrists. He must not be quite as stupid as he looks (which is, to be clear, a very low bar), because he searches me, confiscating the bobby pins, and tosses my backpack out of reach. He pats me clumsily on the head as he leaves, pausing only to flick something into the fireplace. A matchstick, maybe, or a long wooden splinter.

And then I'm all alone, except for the ashes of my spindle and the questions I can't answer, and the coldly comforting thought that the queen didn't underestimate me after all.

❋ ❋ ❋

YOU WOULDN'T THINK a person could fall asleep with their arms cuffed above their head and their neck dangling at a sickening angle, but I'm here to tell you they can.

I wake some hours later to find the light slanting long and heavy through the window and the queen sitting once more in her chair. She's fiddling with something in her lap, and her face looks different in the absence of hunger or hatred: younger, softer.

I try to move my fingers and make a tiny wheeze of pain.

She doesn't look up. "Good morning. Or rather, good evening." I guess she's switched to good cop mode. She holds a little golden object up to the light before setting it gently on the floor beside me. It's my mockingbird, dented and battered but whole once more. "It's a clever little device. Took me the whole afternoon to put it right."

I got that mockingbird from a twelfth-level artificer in a steampunk version of Sleeping Beauty; I doubt very much that a short-tempered medieval witch could repair it. I attempt a sneer, but my lip cracks and bleeds. "If you fixed it, how come it isn't singing?"

"Because I mean you no harm."

I make a noise of pure disbelief and the queen's eyes flash beneath those lowered lashes. She moves. There's a silver gleam, a rush of air, and then there's a wicked point pressing into the bare skin above my collarbone. The little bird breaks into a shrill song, somehow even less melodic than before. Apparently she really did fix it. Under the circumstances—with her knife at my throat—I find my capacity for admiration is somewhat limited.

The queen drags the knife up my neck, scraping along my jugular, pushing uncomfortably into the soft meat beneath my jaw. My chin lifts reluctantly. Her eyes burn into mine, scornful, scorching. "When I threaten your life, I promise you will know it."

I glare back, unflinching, deliberately unimpressed, until the queen's jaw tightens. She sits back with a faint *hnnh* and tucks the knife back into the red drape of her dress. The mockingbird warbles into silence once more.

"I was hoping," she says, with a sweetness entirely at odds with the clenched muscle of her jaw, "that you and I could start again. Here."

She sweeps to her feet and turns a key in my manacles. My arms flop gracelessly to the floor, the fingers swollen and useless as minnows gone belly-up in the bucket.

The queen leaves me clumsily rubbing at my own limbs while she settles beside the fire. There's a second chair across from her and a small table heaped high with food between them. "Come. Help yourself."

I'd like to be prideful and heroic about it, but I haven't eaten in a full day and it's not like I'm going anywhere with dead fish for arms. I stumble into the chair and make a clumsy grab for a pewter cup. You never realize how good water tastes until you've spent a day hungover and chained to a wall.

She waits until I've made it through a full pitcher and three rolls before she speaks. "Let me state my position more clearly." Her voice is earnest, her face carefully contrite. She definitely noticed me noticing her—again, sue me—because her makeup has been carefully reapplied and the laces of her dress tightened so that her breasts are squashed higher. I wonder if this is how she seduced poor Snow White's dad out of his kingdom, and if she even knows who she is when she's not playing the bloodthirsty villain or the helpless femme.

"I am a foreigner and a widow, with nothing but a throne to protect me. But I know now that I will lose that throne, along with my life. And I . . ." She places one hand on what, I am mortified to report, can only be described as her *heaving bosom*. "I need your help, Zinnia Gray."

I skip the apples on the tray and reach for a fourth roll instead. "Again, if you wanted my help, the manacles were not an amazing start."

Another little flash of annoyance, but her voice remains penitent. "A mistake, born out of great need. I'm sorry."

I pick bread from between my molars. "So that mirror of yours. What's it do?"

I can almost hear her teeth grinding. "It shows the truth."

"Where'd you get it?" My voice is casual, my eyes on her face.

"I didn't *get* it. I made it. A woman in my position needs to know the truth at all times." There's the faintest blush of pride in her voice. I count magical objects in my head—comb, bodice lace, poison apple, mirror, my own mockingbird—and decide to believe her. It's a pity she mostly uses her considerable skills for homicide.

"Neat," I say. "Now, can I have my pack?" Suspicion is obvious on her face. I turn both hands palm up. "No, for real, I have to take my meds—magic potions, whatever—twice a day. You'll recall the terminal illness I mentioned."

"That was not a ruse?"

"I mean, yes, it was"—and so is this—"but it's also true. Now give me my shit unless you want me to drop dead in the next twenty minutes." That's horseshit, of course. These days I forget my meds for weeks at a time, approaching them with the sporadic guilt that inspires people to buy multivitamins. It's weird, actually, after living for so long under a strict regimen of pharmaceuticals and appointments, injections and X-rays. I used to be visibly, obviously sick in a way that made parents look away from me in grocery stores, as if my very existence was a bad omen. But now I mostly pass as a healthy person, carrying the GRM like an ugly secret, a bad seed in my belly. It's almost a relief to announce it like this, even if it's mostly a lie.

I snap my fingers and the queen's mouth thins—God, I love bossing around royalty—but she fetches my backpack and tosses it into my lap. I make a show of fishing out ziplock baggies and plastic boxes labeled with days of the week, surreptitiously shoving the mirror deeper into my bag.

The queen watches me count pills into my palm. "What is the nature of this . . . illness?"

I swallow a lump of steroids and blood thinners. "Did you read that whole book of fairy tales?"

A regal nod.

I make a ta-da gesture at my own chest. "You're looking at the protagonist of a bleak contemporary version of Aarne-Thompson tale type 410." My smile tastes bitter. "Little Brier-Rose."

"The . . . pro-tagonist?"

"The main character. In 'Little Brier-Rose,' the protagonist is Brier-Rose."

The queen breathes an *ah* of understanding. She steeples her fingers and says delicately, "In that case, I would imagine you would have a certain sympathy with my situation—"

I cut her off. "And the book. Where'd you get that?"

She's visibly annoyed now, the edges of her innocent act fraying badly, but her voice is still measured. "It appeared three days ago on my shelf."

"No shit?"

Her brows lower several centimeters, in offense or worry. "It is not the only strange appearance in recent months. The cook found a golden egg in the belly of a goose she cut open for dinner, and a fortnight ago, the huntsman said he met a wolf in the woods."

"I mean, isn't that where wolves should be?"

"It . . ." The queen looks pained. "Spoke to him."

"Huh." Am I in some kind of fairy tale mash-up? Is Chris Pine about to pop out and sing Sondheim lyrics in a confused accent?

The queen gathers herself with the expression of a woman who is determined to regain the reins of the conversation. "People do not like strange things. Golden eggs, talking wolves . . . They are seen as ill omens, portents. Acts of witchcraft." Her eyes flicker. "They will soon want a witch to burn."

I make a show of looking around her workroom, with its skulls and pestles and unpleasant things floating in jars. "They won't have to look very hard, will they?"

A flat look. "Quite. And if that book is to be believed, the people will get exactly what they want. You understand why I want out."

And honestly, I do. I've spent most of my life trying to dodge the third act of my story, and the rest of it trying to save other sleeping beauties from theirs; I know exactly how it feels to find yourself hurtling toward a horrible ending.

The difference is what Dr. Bastille would call an issue of *agency*. I steeple my fingers. "Or—and I know this is a big leap for you—you could just stop trying to murder your stepdaughter. It would save everyone a lot of grief."

The queen's face flattens further, her mouth a grim red slash.

"Ah, I see. The chickens are already on their way back home to roost, then. How long has Snow White been in her glass coffin?"

The lips peel reluctantly apart. "A long time."

"Bummer." I throw the word at her with the same pitiless stare she gave me.

She doesn't seem to find it as flattering as I did, because she says in a harsh monotone, "And do you know how my story ends?"

I elect not to explain about institutions of higher education and the department of folklore. "Snow White marries the prince who fell in love with a dead child in the woods—I mean, my story is yikes, but that's double, maybe triple yikes—and they live happily ever after."

"*My* story, I said." Her lips twist in an expression that's only distantly related to a smile and her voice acquires the stilted rhythm of recitation. "*Then they put a pair of iron shoes into burning coals—*"

"You don't have to—"

"*They were brought forth with tongs and placed before her. She was forced to step into the red-hot shoes and dance until she fell down dead.*" She stares hard at me when she finishes, the lines on either side of her mouth like a pair of bleak parentheses.

I stare back, trying not to look grossed out. "Sure, yeah, the German peasantry liked a good comeuppance." Or at least, the Grimms did. There were plenty of other stories floating around the European countryside at the time—weirder, darker, stranger, sexier stories—but the Grimms weren't anthropologists. They were nationalists trying to build an orderly, modern house out of the wild bones of folklore.

"And you think that's *justice*? That I should die dancing in red-hot shoes?" The queen's voice is trembling very slightly, her fingers curling into the wooden arms of her chair.

"No, I mean, I'm not a capital punishment person—my mom's into the prison abolition movement"—she's into all kinds of activism these days, as if all the energy she'd been reserving to hate Big

Energy on my behalf had been redistributed to every other modern supervillain—"but this feels like a 'live by the sword, die by the sword' situation, you know?"

The queen stares at me for a murderous moment, then closes her eyes. "Help me." I didn't think a whisper could sound so imperious.

"If I were begging for my life, I might add a question mark and a 'please.'"

Her eyes remain tightly shut, as if she fears she will throttle me if she sees my face. "Help me, please." She doesn't quite manage the question mark.

I lean forward across the table, drawing out a long, vicious pause before I say, "Nah."

The queen's eyes fly open. Her face is so bloodless her lips look oversaturated, a little unreal. "*Why?*"

"Because I'm not setting an evil queen loose in the multiverse! Because somewhere in the woods right now there's a little girl stuck in an enchanted sleep for no reason except your malice, your *vanity*." I'm aware that I'm no longer playing it cool, that my voice is shaking with honest vitriol, but I can't seem to stop. "She didn't deserve it, she deserved to grow up, to meet a normal dude and live a normal life, to just *live*—"

I bite the inside of my cheek hard, but it's too late. The queen's eyes are alight, her smile small and red. "Oh, Little Brier-Rose, you feel *sorry* for her. Poor Snow White, so pretty, so pure." She shakes her head, mock-pity on her face. "You think this is *her* story."

The queen leans closer over the table, her lips peeling away from her teeth. "You know nothing, Zinnia Gray of Ohio."

The first wobbly notes of mockingbird-song are rising and I'm getting ready to flip the food tray in her lap and make a run for it when there's a hard knock at the door.

The huntsman's voice comes clear and cheerful. "My Queen, a messenger has come from across our borders. You are invited to a royal wedding this very evening!"

✤ ✤ ✤

THE ROOM GOES very still, except for the shallow sound of the queen's breathing, the tick of her pulse in her throat. The two of us sit like awkward statuary until the huntsman prompts doubtfully, "My Queen?"

Her throat makes a small, dry rasp as she swallows. "A wedding," she repeats.

"Yes, Majesty. This very evening!" The huntsman is afflicted with exclamation points too. "Shall I give the messenger your answer to his invitation?"

"Not . . . yet." The queen is paling, wilting before my eyes. She looks suddenly much younger, and it occurs to me for the first time that every queen was once a princess.

"Oh." A scuffing sound on the other side of the door, like a large man shuffling his feet. "It's just, he's waiting in the great hall now, and he brought so many guards with him to escort you, and—"

The queen summons enough regality to say, firmly, "Offer them food and drink while I make myself ready."

"Yes, Majesty."

When there are no subsequent boot steps, she adds, "That will be *all*, Berthold."

"Yes, Majesty." He clomps dutifully down the hall.

The queen still hasn't moved. Her skin is the grayish-white of last week's snow, or cheap dentures. She could almost be mistaken for the protagonist of this story if it weren't for the cold metal crown on her brow. I could almost feel sorry for her if she hadn't poisoned a child and shackled me to a wall.

"*Berthold*, huh?" I slouch back in my chair, ankles crossed, eyebrows up. "He seems bright."

She answers absently, one shoulder twitching in a shrug. "He has his uses."

"*Oh*, it's like that?"

I'm being a dick on purpose, maybe trying to provoke her into anything other than this congealed panic, but her expression barely flickers. "Do you have any idea how difficult it is to find a lover who isn't angling for the throne? He was . . ." Her lip curls, and I can't tell if it's the huntsman or herself she disdains more. "Kind."

It doesn't seem very helpful to remind her that he betrayed her and let Snow White live, so I don't say anything.

Eventually the queen gathers herself, blinking twice and exhaling sharply. If she were a knight, I imagine she would lower her visor, but since she's an evil queen, she stands and stalks to her workbench.

It takes less than a second for her to whirl back to face me. "Where is it? What have you done with it?"

A brief, hissed exchange follows, wherein I try and fail to deflect her accusations ("Where's what?" "You know what, you thieving pustule!" "Okay, calm your tits, it's in my backpack." "Calm my *what*?"), and then she's clutching the tarnished frame of her mirror, whispering to it. I can't hear the words, but I don't have to. Maybe it's in the original German, or maybe it's the Grimms' translation: *Mirror, mirror in my hand, who is the fairest in the land?*

In Sleeping Beauty stories, I've come to recognize certain moments—tropes, you might call them, repeated plot points—that have an echo to them. Pieces of the story that have been told so many times they've worn the page thin: the christening curse, the pricked finger, the endless sleep, the kiss. You can almost feel reality softening around you, at those times.

I feel it now, as the wicked stepmother whispers to her mirror.

I don't know what she sees in the glass, but the queen's throat moves as she swallows. "It's too late."

"Yeah." I make a face, hissing through my teeth. "I recommend you decline this invitation." It never made much sense why the wicked queen showed up at Snow White's wedding, anyway.

A scathing glance in my direction. "Do you really think I have a choice? Do you think she sent all those men as an honor guard?"

I shift in my seat, stomping the tiny worm of pity in my stomach. "So pull some witchy shit. Disguise yourself. Knot your sheets together and climb out the window. Run."

"That would buy me days, maybe weeks. And even if I somehow escaped her reach, what would I do? Hide in a little house in the woods, rotting away?"

The pity vanishes. "Oh, you mean like Snow White did? To escape *you*?"

Her eyes narrow to vicious slits. She says, "I. Have. To. Get. Out," with extra periods between each word.

"That's what I just said." But I know that's not what she means. I reach, not very casually, for the straps of my backpack.

The queen stalks toward me, the mirror still clenched in one hand, the air thickening around her. Stray hairs lift in an invisible breeze, tangling like dark branches across the cold moon of her face. "You will tell me how it's done." This time it's not a question or an order; it's a promise.

So, okay, it was exciting to find myself in a different fairy tale, to feel for the first time the possibility of diverging from my own dreary road, but it's time to go. I stumble out of my chair, backing away, running my free hand against the shelves in search of something, anything sharp. A knife, a splinter, a tooth, a shard of bone. There's nothing.

The queen is close now. She reaches for my collar and twists it in one clawed fist, drawing us together. I can see the plain bones of her face beneath the creams and cosmetics, the hard line of her lips.

And I have no spindle and no tower, no roses or fairies or handsome princes, but I have a monarch close enough to kiss. It'll have to be enough.

I straighten my spine and tilt my face recklessly upward—and, oh God, I have to stand on tiptoe to close the last inch between us, which is both embarrassing and embarrassingly hot—and kiss her.

It's an undeniably weak kiss: a nonconsensual crush of lips and teeth that I would feel pretty bad about if she hadn't been on the verge of nonconsensually torturing me. She breaks away, of course—but not instantly. There's a tiny but critical delay, a moment that makes me wonder how long it's been since the queen met someone outside of her control, and if she might harbor a low taste for sickly, sarcastic peasants.

Then she's glaring and panting, reaching for her knife while her cheeks turn patchy pink. I shouldn't care, because I should be disappearing right now.

Except I'm not.

Nothing is happening. The world is not thinning around me, the infinite pages of the universe are not rustling past. It didn't work, and both of us are extremely screwed.

Something draws the queen's eyes away from me. She looks more closely at the mirror in her hand, and her eyes go wide.

She drops my collar and catches my hand instead. Before I can pull away—before I can even begin to form the word *hey!*—she presses our hands to the glass surface of her mirror.

Except there is no glass. Just our hands, falling into nothing at all.

4

It's COLD, BETWEEN worlds. There's no air, but it whips past me, smelling of frost and first snows. The only warm thing is the queen's hand locked tight around mine, dragging us into a story that doesn't belong to either of us.

My knees hit earth, moss-pillowed and green, and the queen falls beside me with a squashy thud. She makes a sound like air leaking out of a tire, and I'd make fun of her if I didn't feel the same way. My cells are frazzled, as if my entire body was recently microwaved, and it takes me longer than it should to stand and look around.

Trees. Soft, springtime air. Extremely melodic birdsong. The whole scene has a strange haziness to it, like a pre-Raphaelite painting or an old VHS tape.

The queen staggers to her feet in front of me and spreads her hands wide in triumph. "I didn't need you after all, Zinnia Gray. I saved *myself*, as I always have and always will."

I roll my eyes so hard it hurts a little. "Oh yeah? Then who's *that*?"

The queen's victorious smile sags a little at the edges. She follows my gaze over her left shoulder, where a glass coffin lies between the trees. A girl with a cute black bob is lying beneath the glass, her face lit by a single, perfect sunbeam, her hands folded limply around a bouquet of flowers.

The queen stares. She opens her mouth, closes it, and opens it again. "I don't know," she answers.

"Are you serious? Did you hit your head?"

"No, I know who it is, but—" The queen swallows, her eyes fixed on the unsettling white of the girl's face. "That's not *my* Snow White."

"Yeah, I didn't think so." I tuck both hands in my pockets, squinting around at the scenery. "Your world was a little more Gothic, but this place has a 'now-in-Technicolor' vibe." I can tell she doesn't understand, so I say meanly, "Congratulations, you made it to a different world! But you're still in the same story."

The queen looks dazed, staring down at Snow White with the beginnings of revulsion creeping into her eyes. "Why is the light like this?" She reaches her hand tentatively into the sunbeam. Something violet drifts into her palm. "Are there *flower petals* falling over her?"

I don't answer because I'm busy sidling behind her. I snatch the mirror out of the queen's hand and fling it sideways at the trunk of a tree. I'm hoping for a dramatic shatter of glass, but the frame just *thwumps* disappointingly against the bark and falls to the ground, perfectly whole. There's a half second's held breath before both of us dive for the mirror.

The queen shoves past me and I tackle her around the waist. It devolves quickly into a wrestling match, our clothes streaked with moss and dirt, our breath coming fast.

The queen is stronger and meaner than me. "*No*," she pants. "I am—not"—she pins me between her knees and lunges for the mirror—"staying here!"

I try to slap the mirror out of her grip but she turns the glass to meet my hand, and it flies through it, passing back into that cold nowhere.

The last thing I hear is the queen laughing.

❀ ❀ ❀

THIS TIME WE land somewhere dim and damp, like one of those basements that never quite dries out. Opening my eyes takes more effort than it should, and I can't tell whether it's the GRM or the unwilling trips through nowheresville.

The first thing I see is a stranger's face smiling down at me. It's a cute face: freckled and gap-toothed, framed by tangled hair the color of coal. Her lips aren't red as blood and her skin has seen too much sun to be compared to snow, but I know a protagonist when I see one. "Hi," I rasp.

"Good morning!" God save me from princesses and their exclamation points.

"Morning. Where's—" I sit up abruptly, blinking the room into focus. But it's not a room. It's a cave, with a sandy floor and tidy fire pit.

The girl—woman, really, she's got at least a decade on the cherubic kid in the coffin—settles cross-legged beside me. "Your angry woman?" She has a burbling, throaty sort of accent.

"She's not my—yeah, her."

She gestures with her chin toward the entrance of the cave, where more than a dozen men are struggling against a tall, dark-haired figure. There seems to be a lot of swearing from all parties.

"Who are those guys?"

The stranger smiles fondly at them. "Mine. They took me in when my mother tried to murder me, and I've been here ever since." She confides this without much concern, as if attempted filicide is one of life's little misfortunes.

"Ah." My brains feel like hot cheez whiz, but I distantly remember versions of Snow White where she's adopted by robbers or brigands rather than dwarves. Spanish, maybe? Or Flemish? Either way, I'm pretty sure her mom takes another shot at her, and she deserves a heads up. "Listen, Snow White," I begin.

"Sneeuwwitje."

"Listen, Sneeuwwitje—"

The queen shrieks from the cave entrance. "Zinnia! Tell these ruffians to unhand me!"

I shout back without turning, "Tie her up tight, boys, she's super dangerous." There are muffled sounds of fury in response, a definite uptick in swear words.

I try again. "You might already know this, Sneeuwwitje, but your mom is definitely going to try to kill you again. So if anybody shows up with an apple, or a comb, or whatever, just say no."

Sneeuwwitje nods solemnly. "She gave me a demon's ring, which sent me into a deep sleep. How did you know?"

I squint at the stained leather of her clothing, the calluses across her palms. "If she already put you to sleep . . . how come you aren't married to a prince right now?"

"Oh, I told him no. I have seventeen husbands already." An extremely compelling dimple appears, presenting a convincing argument that a man might share one-seventeenth of this woman and count himself lucky. "Eighteen just seemed greedy."

"Sure, yeah," I say faintly, making a distant mental note that not all princesses need saving.

Someone shouts a warning. Footsteps pound across the sand. The queen's fingers close around my ankle and she grins fiercely up at me, a doubled trail of blood leaking from her nose and a mirror in her hand.

I have time to say, "Oh, for fuck's sa—" before the world dissolves again.

❁ ❁ ❁

THE NEXT WORLD has the sleek, blue-lit aesthetic of far-future science fiction. The walls are stacked with cold metal coffins. Waxen faces stare from their small, frosted windows, dead or sleeping, their lips a sickening, poisonous red.

The queen hisses between her teeth and flings us back into the void.

We land on a steep and lonely mountainside. For a moment I think we're alone, but then a branch cracks. A long-legged dog trots past us, its coat silken silver, its eyes fixed on some invisible purpose. Six more follow at its heels, a soft river of paws and skulls and sterling fur.

"*What*—" the queen begins, but a woman comes loping into the view after the dogs. She has hair the color of the moon and a dress the color of snow, and her eyes widen when they land on the queen. For a moment I think she might bare her teeth or set her hounds on us, but then her eyes slide to me. She bows her head, as one would to a fellow soldier in a long war, and runs on after her dogs.

The two of us are left standing together in the pine-scented silence, unsure whether we've been blessed or cursed. The queen takes my hand almost gently this time, before she lifts the mirror again.

A college campus full of ivy-eaten buildings and signs in Korean, where one extremely beautiful boy is offering an apple to another equally beautiful boy.

A sumptuous wedding feast that seems to involve seven ogres and a princess in a gown of richest red.

A hunched woman offering a comb to a little girl, her lips curving in a cold smile.

I can feel myself coming undone, unspooling into the endless whirl of dead girls and coffin lids, wicked mothers and poison apples. The same story repeated again and again, like a woman standing between two mirrors, reflected into infinity.

And then another forest, curled and black beneath a starless sky. I wrench my arm away from the queen and pluck the mirror from her other hand. She's too weak to stop me, her skin clammy and chilled, her limbs shuddering.

She rolls onto her stomach beside me, panting into the dark muck of leaves and earth. "This is where you draw the line?" she spits. "*This is where you choose to stay?*"

She has an extremely good point. The woods around us bear no resemblance at all to the first forest we landed in, with its flower petals and birdsong. The trees here are knotted and bent, like snapped bones that have healed poorly, and the darkness is the kind that makes your eyes ache if you look at it too long. I've hit a couple of versions of Sleeping Beauty that edged into horror, and returned with new scars and probably some undiagnosed PTSD. Charm threw a fit about it, and the next time I left home I found a new pocketknife and a first aid kit in my pack, along with a note reading *Don't die, bonehead* in Prim's fancy calligraphy.

So, no, I don't love the Grimm-dark vibe of these woods, but I'm tired on a subatomic level, my muscles shaking and my teeth chattering, and I'm done channel surfing at someone else's whim. "Why not?" I make an effort to crawl away and manage several consecutive feet before collapsing against my own backpack, mirror still in my hand. "Look, you've got to give it a rest. You're going to kill yourself at this pace."

"As if you care about my fate." Her voice darkens, silky and low. "Beyond your base desires, of course."

"My what?"

The queen raises herself to her hands and knees just so she can do a haughty glare at me. "It's a little late to feign indifference. You *kissed* me."

I'm torn between explaining that my kiss was actually a failed escape attempt and clarifying that there's nothing especially base about desiring a tall, dangerous woman with terrible vibes (whomst among us, etc.). Instead, I say, "Whatever. I just need a break from that mirror, okay?"

"Then tell me how to get out of this damned story." The queen's voice is ragged, pushed far beyond exhaustion but still unwilling to bend. It would be admirable if it weren't extremely annoying. "Tell me, and I swear I'll stop."

"Bite me."

"Now is not the time for your crude fantasies!" She climbs unsteadily to her feet, takes two wavering steps in my direction. "You have no idea what it's like to fight for your own right to exist. To know yourself doomed, yet to keep striving—"

I throw a wad of leaves at her. "Cry me a fucking river, woman. You just found out how your story ends *last week*. I've spent my whole life under a death sentence."

The queen is clawing wet leaves out of her hair, teeth flashing white in the gloom. "You think I haven't?" Her voice is a strangled hiss. "I may not have known about the iron shoes, but I was always headed for a bad ending. I was an ugly second daughter with uncanny power, and then I was a foreign bride who bore no heirs. Now I am a queen who is feared only slightly more than she is hated, and my time is up. But I have fought tooth and nail to survive, and no pretty little princess is going to stop me."

This little monologue leaves me with two not entirely comfortable sensations. The first is the sudden, lurching shame of my worldview being wrenched out of shape as it occurs to me that Snow White might not be the only victim here. The second comes from the word *pretty*, which the queen tried to hurl at me like a slap, but which faltered mid-flight and landed quite differently. I find myself struggling to form a sufficiently scathing response, or any response at all.

But she's not even looking at me anymore. She's staring into the abyssal black between the trees with a long-suffering expression. "Oh, not another one."

There's a fragile amber light flickering closer, like a candle held in a shaking fist. Scurrying footsteps. The terrified panting of someone running for reasons that are not recreational.

The queen looks inclined to melt into the shadows and let this character pass us by, their narrative uninterrupted, but I stand woozily and say, "Hello?"

I catch a glimpse of a young girl with brown skin and terror-struck eyes before I realize the lantern has left her night-blind. She slams into my diaphragm and we go down in a pile of limbs and elbows while the queen gives a small, pained sigh.

The girl scrambles to her knees, already trying to launch herself back into the tangled dark of the woods, but I catch her shoulder. "Hey, it's okay. We're not going to hurt you."

She shrugs my hand away. "I have to hide—they're coming—"

"Who? The huntsman?"

She nods, wheeling to look behind her as if she expects to find a henchman lumbering out from behind a tree. The woods are perfectly still.

I know she'll be all right on her own—she's due to find a friendly bunch of dwarves or fairies soon, and the huntsman probably isn't even chasing her—but she's a lot younger than the other Snow Whites we've seen, and much more frightened. I find myself saying, "Don't worry, we'll help you find a safe place."

The queen makes a strangled noise of protest and I shoot her a repressive look. "*Won't* we?"

"I don't see why I should," she huffs.

"God, you're the *worst.*"

"You think you're such a hero, but you won't help me—"

"Maybe if you acted just a *smidge* less evil I'd consider it."

The queen lunges, fangs bared, but I raise her mirror and waggle it warningly. "Ah-ah. You wouldn't want to break this, now would you?"

It's at this point, when the queen's face is a twisted rictus of fury, her eyes fixed on her precious mirror, that the young girl shoves between us.

She raises her lantern high and says, "I'll find it myself," over one shoulder as she passes us.

I pause long enough to give the queen a "now look what you did" face before hurrying after Snow White. I rummage in my pack one-handed and produce a battered wooden box. "Here, this'll tell us where to go." I open the compass and wait for the needle to wobble to a stop, directing us northeast.

The girl leads the way, striding past humped roots and clawing branches, and I follow her without consulting the queen, because it's not like she'll let either me or the mirror out of her sight. We haven't made it ten paces before I hear her stomping and muttering after us.

The woods darken and thicken around us. Briars tug at our clothes and small, slinking creatures rustle just past the bright ring of lantern light. A few reluctant stars blink like filmy eyes through the branches, but the moon refuses to rise.

The young Snow White never slows down or hesitates. I wonder briefly what could scare a kid like this, who walks so fearlessly through the dark, and decide I'd rather not know.

Eventually another light shines through the trees: a pair of lit windows, warm and inviting, wildly out of place in the thorned and twisted wood.

I point Snow White toward the windows. "Okay, there's probably somebody in there who can help you out. Just do whatever they say and stay away from strangers, and you'll . . . be . . ." I trail away, because there's a small bird silhouetted in one of the windows, the first we've heard or seen all night. Something about the shape of it rings a very distant and unlikely bell in my head.

It flutters toward us and perches directly above me, lit from below by the shuddering yellow of Snow White's lantern. It fixes me with a single bright and clever eye and I know, suddenly, where I've seen this bird before.

I whisper, softly and a little desperately, because this is more than six impossible things and breakfast is still a long way off, "No way."

But the multiverse in all its infinite weirdness, answers: *Yes way.*

The door of the hut opens and an old woman stands in the spill of light looking exactly as she did five years ago, when I sat at her table drinking tea with a different Disney princess.

I feel dizzy, suddenly uncertain, as if I might have fallen into the gap between stories and gotten stuck. "Z-Zellandine?"

Zellandine, for her part, does not look even slightly surprised to see me. She points her chin inside the hut and says tiredly, "Well, come on, then."

5

It's the young Snow White who moves first. She strides into the fairy's house with a stiff spine and an expression suggesting that nothing in front of her could possibly be worse than whatever's behind her. Zellandine welcomes her with a grandmotherly nod, gesturing to a seat around the table. There's a rightness to the shape they make against the light, two silhouettes repeated in a thousand variations of a thousand stories: the old woman welcoming the weary traveler, the witch inviting the child inside, the fairy godmother sheltering the maiden.

Then Zellandine turns back to us and the rightness vanishes. We eye one another—three straying characters who have run off the rails of their own stories and collided in someone else's—before Zellandine grimaces as if to say *What a mess*, and chucks her head toward the other three chairs around the table.

Her hut is exactly as I remember it, cottagecore with a witchy edge, blue-glass bottles on the shelves and herbs strung before a crackling fireplace. The only difference is that the kitchen table has four chairs now, and four cups of tea on mismatched saucers.

We sip our tea in uncertain silence, not looking at one another. Zellandine butters bread and sets it in front of our Snow White, who eats with the determined efficiency of someone who doesn't turn down free calories. In the fuller light of the hut she looks even younger than I thought, her cheeks still gently rounded, but she lacks a little kid's wide-eyed trust. Her expression is closed and watchful, precocious in the bleak, uncanny way of a child who has spent too much time thinking about how and when she'll die. It's the expression I'm wearing in every one of my school photos.

"You'll find a bed made, upstairs," Zellandine tells her gently.

Snow White's eyes cut to the bright-lit windows, shining like beacons into the black sea of trees, and Zellandine adds, even more gently, "I'll keep watch tonight."

Snow White nods in grave thanks, one hand on her chest, then repeats the motion to me and—after a moment's hesitation—the queen. The queen's eyes widen very slightly. I suppose wicked stepmothers aren't often thanked.

Zellandine clears the cups as Snow White climbs the steps to the loft, which I'm 98 percent sure didn't exist the last time I had tea in this hut. "There are three beds up there," Zellandine observes.

The queen makes a visible effort to un-slump herself from the table. "I thank you, but I'm afraid Zinnia and I must be on our way." Her tone aspires toward chilly rebuke, but lands closer to *very tired*.

"Oh my God, give it a *rest*." I tap the silver frame of her mirror on the tabletop. "You can get back to your jailbreak first thing in the morning. I promise."

Even her venomous glare is exhausted. After a long and weighty pause, she grates, "Your word that you will neither flee nor damage the mirror while I rest."

I'm tempted to roll my eyes, but I restrain myself to a flat stare. "Sure, yeah. Scout's honor." I slide the mirror across the table and she stops it with two long fingers against the frame, her lips slightly parted in shock. "See what you get when you ask nicely?"

The queen cuts me a look, dark and inscrutable, before following Snow White upstairs.

"Sorry about her," I say to Zellandine. "She's the villain, obviously."

Zellandine unties her apron, fingers slower and older than I remember them, and settles across from me. "Oh, we villains aren't all bad." A flash of humor in the pale blue of her eyes.

"No, she's like, a *legit* villain, not a misunderstood protofeminist fairy."

Zellandine makes a very neutral sound, her eyes glinting with that subterranean humor. "We don't all get to choose the parts we're given to play. You should know that better than most."

I think unwillingly of all the other roles the queen was given: the ugly princess, the barren queen, the foreign monarch. A string of women with just enough power to be hated and not quite enough to protect themselves. I swallow a lump of inconvenient sympathy. "Sure, okay, but we all get to choose what we do *next*. A sad backstory is no excuse for being a dick. I should know."

This feels to me like a solid rhetorical win, but Zellandine undermines it by murmuring, "You should, yes," under her breath.

"And what's that supposed to—"

"How's the princess?" Zellandine asks it blandly, even pleasantly; there's no reason the question should feel like a sucker punch.

I try to make my face equally bland and pleasant. "She's good. Fine.

She's married now, actually." My smile feels weird but I can't seem to make it un-weird. "Doing the happily-ever-after thing, I guess."

Zellandine gives me a nod containing more sympathy than is strictly warranted. "So how long has it been since you last saw her?"

"A while. A few months." Six months and twelve days, but whatever. "Anyway, I don't know why it matters. What matters is *what the hell is going on?* What are you *doing* here?"

Zellandine doesn't look even slightly thrown by the topic change; it's annoyingly hard to surprise a prophetic fairy. "I could ask you the same thing," she replies evenly. When I squint, she lifts one shoulder. "This isn't your story either."

"Yeah, well, that's not my fault. I'm headed back to the Sleeping Beauty–verse as soon as I can." I don't mention the secret, wild hope that I don't have to return to my own story at all. That I've found a way to break free of this endless cycle of cursed girls and pricked fingers, to punch through the walls of my own plot and bust into other narrative dimensions like a fairy-tale Kool-Aid Man. And if I can make a new beginning for myself in some other story—what's to stop me making a new ending too?

There's a pause before I can speak through the hope now crawling up my throat. "I was kidnapped by an evil queen. How did *you* get here?"

Zellandine sits back in her chair, watching me as if she knows exactly what I didn't say. "It's happened a few times now. I step outside and find myself in deep woods I've never seen before, on a mountaintop that isn't mine. Once, I woke to find my house all covered in sweets, with gingerbread for shingles and boiled sugar for window panes."

I think: *Oh shit.* I say: "Oh shit." I remember the talking wolf in the queen's world, my juice-stained copy of Grimms' fairy tales, things shaken loose from their moorings and set adrift. "You're slipping between stories."

Zellandine tilts her head. "There do seem to be a lot of tales that require someone old and magical living alone in the woods. I don't mind it, mostly—cursing the occasional haughty prince, letting a handsome knight or two warm themselves by my fire." I check her face for innuendo and find it suspiciously absent. "But it's been happening more and more often. And I'm starting to feel like . . ." She trails away, her hand stroking the inside of her wrist. The flesh there has milky translucence I don't remember from five years before.

"Like butter spread over too much bread?"

"Yes, like that," she breathes. "And I confess, I was fond of my home on the mountainside. We miss it." Her blackbird trills to her, but I hardly notice because the word *home* is rattling between my ribs like a stray bullet, carelessly fired. I think of my phone, fully charged but turned off, zipped in one of those inner backpack pockets no one ever opens. I think of three hands buried in the same popcorn bowl. I think of Charm's face the last time I saw her, asking me for something I couldn't give.

"Well." I clear my throat, searching for levity and finding nothing but sickly sarcasm. "You have to admit, your story kind of sucked."

"But it was mine." Zellandine's tone is sharper than I've heard before, grief-edged. She bites the inside of her cheek before adding, "I might not have chosen it, but I always chose what to do next."

"Often on other people's behalf, if I remember right."

I meant it as a stinging rebuke, but Zellandine is nodding thoughtfully. "To their detriment, I think now. I was trying to save others from a fate like mine, but perhaps I was taking away their own right to choose, to make of their stories what they would."

She gives me such a mild look that I bristle defensively. "Hey, I'm not—it's not like that. I'm helping people fix their stories. And if they can't be fixed, I help them escape."

Zellandine is still looking at me with that weaponized mildness. "Oh, I don't think any of us escape our stories entirely."

"Prim did."

"Did she?" I want to sneer that I don't think Perrault or Disney ever pictured Sleeping Beauty marrying a hot butch with an undercut and a Superman tattoo, except I have this horrible sinking feeling that she might be right. I mean, I said it myself: *She's doing the happily-ever-after thing, I guess.*

I raise my hands in mock-surrender, abruptly exhausted. "Well. I'm sorry about the narrative slippage. But I'm glad you were here tonight." My chair scrapes against wood as I stand and make my way toward the steps.

Zellandine speaks just as my hand lands on the railing. "I don't understand what's happening to me, or how." She turns, her eyes catching the dying red of the hearth, and in that moment I see her as she must be in other stories: the fairy who curses kingdoms, the crone who punishes ungrateful travelers, the witch who waits in the woods.

Her mouth twists, wry and tired, and she is only Zellandine again. "But I think both of us know why."

❖ ❖ ❖

ZELLANDINE'S BEDS ARE squashy and warm, piled deep with flannel and down, but I sleep in fitful bursts. Each time I drift toward unconsciousness I'm woken by some small noise—the scritching of skeletal black branches at the window, the distant shrieks of night birds—and left wide-eyed and panting in a pool of adrenaline. Snow White is apparently accustomed to sleeping through horror movie sound effects, but every time I look toward the queen's bed, I catch the lambent white of open eyes before both of us turn away.

Breakfast the next morning is gray and quiet. I chase my oats in miserable circles, muffling phlegmy coughs in the crook of my elbow and refusing to wonder if they sound wetter than they did yesterday, if tiny protein buds are already sprouting along my bronchial tree like deadly Christmas lights.

The queen doesn't look great either. There are spongy bruises beneath both eyes and her makeup is mostly smeared away, leaving her looking like a painting that sat too long in direct sunlight. Several determined freckles are poking through the remains of her face powder, forming an unexpected constellation.

Zellandine settles at the head of the table and folds her hands in a businesslike manner. "We didn't introduce ourselves properly last night. I'm Zellandine, an old friend of Zinnia's."

She looks expectantly at the queen, who looks, for no reason, at me. For the briefest moment I see something raw and bleeding behind her eyes, like an unstitched wound, before she gathers the edges of herself and presses them back together. "You may call me Your Maj—"

"Eva." I interrupt. The queen gives me a glare that's more searching than scorching. I don't like the vulnerable set of her eyes, another glimpse of that red wound in the middle of her, so I lean over and stage-whisper, "Short for Evil Queen."

While she's still sputtering, I gesture to the poor kid sitting next to me. "And this, of course, is Snow White."

Snow White has been eating her oats in determined silence, looking at the windows as if she's waiting for something to emerge from the trees. At the sound of my voice, she flinches so badly she sends her bowl shattering to the floor. She doesn't seem to notice, crouching in her chair with her eyes pinned on me.

"Oh, my bad," I say mildly. "Is that not your name?"

She answers slowly, as if she half expects me to sprout fangs and pounce. "No. You don't—" Her eyes narrow, moving from my face to my jeans to the backpack propped against my chair. "You're not . . . from here, are you?"

"Nope. I'm an interdimensional tourist, just passing through."

She stares for another long, hard second before saying tersely, "My name is Red."

"Huh." There are several Red-variants running through Western folklore—Rose Red and Little Red, for a start—but I'm not sure what any of them would be doing in a Snow White story. (Yes, there is technically a Grimm story titled "Snow-White and Rose-Red," but it has nothing whatsoever to do with the other Snow White; yes, it is very confusing. Take it up with Jacob and Wilhelm.)

Well. The name Snow White always had uncomfortable implications about racialized standards of beauty; maybe in this world, her mother named her for the drop of blood, rather than the snow it fell on.

"Hi, Red." I say it as comfortingly as I can, which isn't very. "You should be safe now. Zellandine is a powerful fairy, and she'll keep you hidden from your wicked stepmother."

Red's eyebrows scrunch together. "My what?"

"Or mother, or sister, or whoever—"

"Perhaps," Zellandine suggests, with a touch of asperity, "the girl could tell her own story."

After a beat, during which I stick my tongue out at Zellandine and the queen sighs as if she regrets every decision that led her to be sitting at this table, Red does. It takes approximately two sentences to confirm that we are very, very far from the singing woodland creatures and flower-strewn forests of Disney. We're not even in one of the

Grimms' bloody fantasies, with their violent morality; we're some-place darker and wilder and much older, where the villain has a terri-ble hunger, and the hero is the one who survives it.

Red, it turns out, is not a princess. She's a shepherd's daughter from a poor village at the edge of the woods. Every winter, the queen sends her hunters to snatch the strongest and healthiest children and drag them back to her lair.

"Nobody knows what she does with them. Ivy says she gives them candies and jewels, but Ivy's stupid." Red's voice is flat and even. "I think she plucks out their hearts and eats them. Either way, nobody ever sees them again."

A small, appalled silence follows this. It's the queen—Eva, I sup-pose, since she's not the queen of anything around here, and the name seems to annoy her so deeply—who speaks first. "But why would she do that?"

Red gives her a look suggesting the cannibal queen's personal mo-tivations are fairly low on her list of concerns. Zellandine speculates about the latent magical properties of innocent hearts and the power that could theoretically be gained through ingestion, but I miss most of it because I'm busy hissing back and forth with Eva. ("Hold up, Miss Moral High Ground, didn't you ask for Snow White's lungs and liver?" "Yes, but I wasn't going to *eat* them! I'm not *depraved*!")

I shush Eva, which she visibly hates, and turn back to Red. "And your family, your parents—they just let her take you?" I consider Red's hair, pulled away from her face in pretty twists, and remember my dad braiding my hair every day before school, his fingers gentle. Someone must love her. "They didn't fight for you?"

Eva makes a scathing noise that tells me more than I wanted to know about her own parents, but Red answers with a soft and terrible brevity. "They did."

Eva seems to be struggling with something, her lips working until she says, almost angrily, "Why don't you all leave? Or hide?"

"She always finds you," Red says, her voice still soft. "She talks to the moon, people say, or maybe a magic mirror. And then . . ." Her eyes flick to the window again, and this time the warm brown of her skin goes ashen. "And then her huntsman come to fetch you."

There's something funny about the grammar of that sentence, but it's only when I hear the crunch of many pairs of boots through the woods, then the thud of many fists on the door, that I understand I misheard her. She didn't say *huntsman*, with a singular A; she said *huntsmen*.

❁　❁　❁

My FIRST, PROFOUNDLY unhelpful thought is: *This isn't how it goes.* There's supposed to be a witch disguised as an old woman, an apple the color of blood, a pretty coffin in the woods. There's supposed to be three chances and a happy ending. But instead there are fists pounding on the door.

A shrill voice shouts, "We know you're in there, girlie! Come out, queen's orders!"

Red is out of her chair, backing against the counter, fingers curling around a bread knife. Zellandine is rising, tightening her apron with trembling fingers. Only Eva and I remain frozen, like a pair of mannequins in a bustling department store.

By the time Zellandine opens the door, her hands are not shaking at all. "You must be mistaken, good sirs. There's no one here but me." It's a brave effort, and a doomed one. She barely says the words before a thin-faced man shoulders his way past her, eyes roving hungrily around the cottage. More men pour in behind him. They all have the same stringy, unhealthy look, and they all wear the same yellowish necklaces. The necklaces rattle oddly when they move, like chattering teeth. It takes me too long to realize that's what they actually are: human teeth, strung on leather cords. Acid boils in my throat, sick and hot.

The leader points to Red. "Come with us."

She shakes her head once, knuckles pale around her bread knife, chin still high, and God, this kid deserves better than this bloody, brutal story. One of the huntsmen draws a knife of his own, one never intended to slice bread, but it turns abruptly to ash in his hand. Greasy flakes drift silently to the floor.

"I did not invite you across my threshold, boy," Zellandine growls behind him. But she's panting as she says it, the flesh of her face gone white and thin as onionskin. Back in Primrose's world she'd seemed ageless, invincible, a woman who could turn knives into feathers with the slightest flick of her eyelash. But maybe that was only true in her own world, and the rules are different in this one. Maybe power has a price here, and she's paying it.

The knifeless huntsman seems to sense her weakness, because he turns and shoves Zellandine hard, as if she's not a witch but merely an old woman. Someone yells, and it's only once I'm on my feet that I realize it was me. The huntsmen are all staring at me and the strap of my pack is tight in my hand, and it's not like I have a stellar life expectancy anyway. I sling it into the leader's face.

The fight that follows is brief and embarrassing. In less than a minute I'm facedown on the floor with someone's knee ungently separating my vertebrae. A hand snarls in my hair and smacks my face almost perfunctorily against the floor. Everything goes staticky and muffled after that, my vision stippled with black starbursts.

There are boot steps. A fleshy thud and a strangled cry. The head huntsman asking, from far away, "What about you? Going to give us trouble?"

A pause, taut with the promise of violence, followed by Eva's voice speaking a single, thin syllable. "No."

The huntsmen leave then, pausing only to offer a few casual kicks to my rib cage as they pass.

In their absence, the only sound is the steady *splish* of my blood against the floorboards and the whine of the door as it swings in the wind, and—in the distance, fading fast—the cries of a brave little girl who has come, at last, to the end of her bravery.

6

"So, obviously"—my pack whumps onto the tabletop—"we have to go after her."

I'm hoping if I say it with enough calm authority, we can skip the part of the conversation where Eva gets whiny and morally gray about it, but apparently not, because she says, "I assure you we do not," without even opening her eyes. Her hands are propped on the kitchen counter, her head hanging low. Her fancy braids are hanging loose down the back of her neck now, nothing at all like the sleek black crown she wore when I first saw her in the mirror.

"I mean, I agree, ideally there would be more of us, and Zellandine would be conscious." After my ears had stopped ringing and my nosebleed had slowed to a jellied ooze, I bullied Eva into helping me scoop the fairy off the floor. I have no idea how we would have gotten her up the stairs, but luckily we didn't have to. The steps had vanished, replaced by a single bed in the corner, the sheets already turned down. We tucked Zellandine under the covers and received a wan smile in return. Her cold fingers covered mine. "You'll go after her, won't you?" she asked resignedly. I nodded. The fingers tightened. "But afterward—go *home*. Things are tangling, the lines are blurring. You can't keep running forever." My second nod was more of a non-committal jerk of my chin. Zellandine's eyes narrowed. "Every story ends, Zinnia."

She appears to be sleeping now, her blackbird perched on the bed-post, considering her with one worried eye and then the other.

"But you know what they say." I give the queen a hearty shrug. "If wishes were fishes."

Eva opens her eyes then, but only to squint at me as if she has a sudden headache. "Then what?"

I consider. "Never mind. The point is, we have to go."

Her mouth hardens. Her eyes close again. "No, we don't."

I'm unpacking and repacking my backpack, dispensing with un-necessary weight. I unzip an inner pocket and lay my phone carefully on the table. "You know," I say, trying very hard—medium hard—well, a little—to keep my tone polite, "maybe we wouldn't have to go save a kid from a cannibal queen if you'd put up literally any fight at all, but you chose to *sit* there while the rest of us—"

Now Eva spins to face me, lips curling away from her teeth. "And what did that get you, exactly?" She closes the distance between us and reaches abruptly for my face. I stare her down, refusing to flinch or look away, but her thumb brushes with surprising softness across my chin. It comes away smeared with glutinous red. "I have tried be-fore to explain my position, but perhaps you did not understand." Her voice vibrates, thick with emotion. "Everything I have done, every-thing I will do, serves one purpose: to *survive*."

And there is an un-small part of me that understands that, and more than understands it. Sympathizes with it, admires it, even—

okay, yes—desires it. (The way she looks right now, her eyes blazing with that bottomless life-hunger, her face lit with an intensity that burns straight past prettiness and toward something far more dangerous . . . No jury would convict me.)

But I've tried just surviving. I spent twenty-one years pouring all my want and will toward it, adhering to a set of rules—move fast, go hard, don't fall in love, try not to die—that left me with exactly one friend and zero plans. And in the end, none of it mattered anyway. In the end, it was just me and my nonnegotiable illness, and the only reason I survived was because someone else (a couple of someones, technically) saved me.

So I just look at Eva for a while, in all her selfish, ferocious, sexy will to survive, and shake my head. "Fine." I hold down the power button on my phone and wait for the screen to light up, steadfastly refusing to think why I'm turning it on or who I might call. "But I'm going."

Eva's eyes flicker. *"Why?"*

"Because . . ."

There are noble ways to finish that sentence (because Red is brave and clever and she deserves better; because the hot nerd on *The Good Place* was right, and the meaning of life basically boils down to what we owe to each other) and less noble, potentially more honest ways (because as long as I'm saving other people I can forget, briefly, that I can't save myself; because storming an evil fortress is easier than showing Charm my X-rays and watching her understand, all over again, that I'm not in it for the long haul, that there's still a trolley barreling toward both of us).

I finish boringly. "Just like, because. Someone should."

Eva's expression remains hard and fixed, like a marble statue titled *Monarch Who Is Unmoved by the Pleas of the Peasantry,* but there's an odd wistfulness in her eyes, almost as if she envies me. As if she wishes she, too, were a stupid twenty-six-year-old with the reckless bravery of the terminally ill rather than the predictable villain doing the predictably villainous thing. I think of Zellandine telling me that we don't get to choose our stories, but we get to choose what we do next.

A very bad idea occurs to me then. I slide my arms into my backpack straps and meet her eyes very squarely. "If you come with me and help save Red, I'll tell you how to get out of this story." I lean forward and tap the back of her magic mirror, which is never far from her hand. "For real."

Eva's eyes move from the mirror to my face, widening as she realizes I don't just mean *out of this particular version of this story* but *out of this kind of story more broadly.* Out of her own horrible ending, away from the cruel logic of her character arc.

Her face finally moves, and it takes me a moment to recognize the expression for what it is. I've seen her sneer, and smirk, and bare her teeth in a dozen cruel grins, but this is the first time she's genuinely smiled at me.

I'm obliged to blink several times. "So." There's an answering smile spreading helplessly across my face. "It's a deal?"

❖ ❖ ❖

IN RETROSPECT, IT's possible that Eva and I could have spent more time in the planning stage of our rescue attempt.

All we really did was consult the magic mirror, which confirmed that Red was still alive (Eva had stared at Red's face, terrified and tear-streaked, with something very close to guilt), and shove supplies in my bag. Bottled water and snacks, my cool magic compass, her cool magic mirror, a functioning, fully charged phone, and two of Zellandine's sharpest knives, which we—well, I—fully intended to return.

But after we stepped across the threshold there was a slight, inaudible *pop,* and a rush of wind that smelled very faintly of roses. When we turned around, Zellandine and her hut were gone.

There didn't seem to be anywhere to go after that except onward. I pulled out my compass and thought of Red, with her watchful eyes and her grim mouth, her hair twisted by someone who fought for her and lost. The needle spun southwest, and the two of us followed it.

It was an uneventful journey. Most things—and boy, did this forest have more than its fair share of Things—didn't bother us, either because of the knives or because they were looking for even bigger, juicier Things to eat. Around lunch (half a carrot cake Clif Bar apiece, which Eva considered with scientific curiosity, palpating it gently before realizing she was expected to consume it), something horrible landed on my open pack. It tore at the contents, shredding and shrieking, long talons flashing.

Eva had it pinned to a tree with her knife through its heart before I could properly scream. I would tell you what kind of animal it was, but I have no idea, and looking at it made my brain cramp. So I'll just say it was bad. Like, if a snake fucked a tarantula and their baby died in a tar pit and was later reanimated by a necromancer who graduated at the absolute bottom of his class.

"Thanks," I said in a voice that was a mere two octaves higher than usual.

I received nothing in response but a contemptuous curl of Eva's upper lip. But both of us moved more carefully after that, and startled at small noises. By the time dusk settled over the woods—although I'm not convinced it's ever fully not-dusk here; it seems to exist on a limited palette ranging from gloaming to gloomy—we were shivery and tense, and I'd spent the last several miles trying and failing to think of a funny name for the twitch in my left eye.

Eva held up her hand and I flinched backward. "What, where—"

She was pointing silently through the trees. I followed the line of her finger and saw it: a high stone wall stained a viscous, tarry black. I looked upward through the dark lace of the leaves, and that was the moment it occurred to me that Eva and I could have prepared better for what struck me now as a laughable attempt at a rescue mission. We could, for example, have brought siege weaponry, or a smallish army, or one of those big mech suits from *Pacific Rim*. Instead, we brought two kitchen knives and an assortment of underpowered magical objects, like video game characters rushing to the boss battle without leveling up.

I say, "Oh, *yikes*," which really undersells the enormity of the yikes we're facing.

I mean, sure, when one is looking for the lair of a cannibal queen, one expects to encounter a certain degree of spookiness. One might anticipate something resembling the Beast's castle pre-makeover, with gargoyles and buttresses and more lightning storms than is statistically likely. One does not anticipate what I'm seeing now, which is a jagged ruin of black glass and bones that makes the Black Gate of Mordor look like the Barbie Malibu Dreamhouse. Trees press against the walls, reaching over the battlements with fawning fingers. Dark, winged things circle the towers, screeching in too-human voices.

"Well." Eva makes a sardonic gesture at the walls. "What are we waiting for?"

After another brief round of hissing ("This was your idea." "I know! There's just like, more skulls than I was expecting! Give me a second."), I gather myself and say calmly, "Okay, there has to be a back way in."

"I very much doubt it. If I built an impregnable fortress to hold my desperate victims, I certainly wouldn't—"

"Yeah, I know, but there's *always* a back way in. Trust me." Eva's face makes a funny flinch, which I can only assume is her natural response to the concept of trust, but she trails huffily behind me as we circle the wall. A few guards go clomping past us along the battlements, but none of them seem to see us creeping below them. I guess this isn't the kind of place that people often try to get into.

After less than fifty feet of sneaking, a damp, foul breeze emerges from somewhere nearby and wafts across us. It smells like old meat and human suffering, and it leads us without much trouble to a rusted, weed-choked grate set in the earth.

I wave my hand and whisper, "Voilà. A back way in."

Eva squints sourly at the sewer grate. She sniffs. "It must be nice. Being the protagonist."

I give her my cheekiest smile and say, "It suits you." It comes out more sincerely than I intended, and Eva's eyes flick to mine, then away.

I haul the grate aside and shimmy down the hole, landing with a fairly repellent plop. The water (it is not water) is sludgy and cold, running halfway up my thighs. It feels like an obvious moment for Eva to cut and run, but she lands beside me without fuss and strides onward, looking—just for a moment, in the dark—a little like a hero.

❁ ❁ ❁

WE WADE THROUGH the muck for just long enough that I'm starting to worry that these sewers function as actual sewers rather than plot devices and don't lead anywhere useful, but then we hear things echoing off the wet stone walls: cries and pleas, the miserable *clink-clink* of chains dragging across stone floors. The unmistakable sounds of a castle dungeon.

There's a grate directly above us, casting a sickly shard of light across Eva's face. I nod upward. "This is our stop."

We slither out into a space that looks like a slightly larger version of the sewer we just left, except that there are greasy torches spitting along the walls and cells with iron bars for doors. Most of them are empty, and some of them contain . . . pieces . . . that I refuse to look at long enough to identify. We pass a cell with actual, live occupants, but my heart sinks when I see that they aren't children.

But one of them is a tall woman with a proud arch to her nose and warm brown skin. The others are slumped listlessly against the walls, but this woman is on her feet, reaching through the bars to wiggle a shard of bone in the lock. Her hair is twisted neatly away from her face.

She gives us a wary once-over as we approach the bars, but apparently we don't look like a threat or salvation. She returns her attention to the lock, manacles clanking softly against the bars.

"You're Red's mom, aren't you." I don't say it like a question, because it isn't one.

At the sound of the word *Red* her eyes snap to my face. "Where is she? Who are you? Did they catch her?"

I hiss the word *"chill"* between clenched teeth, just as a broad-shouldered man stands and sets a hand on the woman's shoulder. She chills, reluctantly, but her eyes are a pair of knives pressed to my jugular.

I decide to be blunt and quick. "The huntsmen took her a few hours ago."

The woman closes her eyes. The big man grunts as if he's taken a physical blow.

"It's okay, we'll save her." I look up and down the dungeon, wishing for my bobby pins. "We'll, uh, we'll find a guard and steal the keys—"

I'm trying to comfort her, but Red's mother isn't listening to me. She's speaking in a calm voice to the big man behind her. "Looks like we're out of time, love."

He sucks air through his teeth. "It'll be loud. Bring them down on us."

"Let them come." Something in her voice makes me think of snapping bones, blood on the walls.

The man tears a seam at the hem of his shirt and withdraws a waxy twist of paper. He unwinds it to reveal a mound of grainy black sand, which he pours neatly into the keyhole. I have the somewhat humbling suspicion that I'm not necessary in this story, that I'm lucky I even got a speaking part.

The woman raises her hands and seems to recall, at the last moment, that Eva and I exist. "Stand back," she says. We do.

She strikes her manacles against the bars, sending showers of angry white sparks over the lock. Once, twice. All the prisoners are standing now, watching her, murmuring to one another. I can feel the weight of their hope like a physical thing, urging her on. I wonder how many of their children were stolen.

On the third strike, a tendril of smoke leaks from the keyhole. Shortly afterward I find myself lying flat on my back with a shrill ringing in my ears. The air smells hot. I think one of my incisors is loose.

I sit up to see Red's mother stepping through the mangled remains of her cell door, black smoke trailing her limbs. She's followed closely by the big dude (Red's dad? I don't want to make assumptions about heteronormative family structures in alternate universes, but the way he shadows Red's mom suggests he belongs to her) and the rest of the villagers. They flock silently around her as if they're waiting for a command, which I guess they are. Red's mother sends the oldest and youngest villagers down into the sewers and assembles the rest into rough formation. She nods once to me, like a commander acknowledging a new recruit, and sets off, heading upward out of the dungeons and into the castle itself.

I feel like I should ask questions, like *where are we going?* or *what happens when the guards turn up?* But Red's mother still has that sharpened bone in her fist, and her father's expression suggests an entire armed battalion would present only a fleeting obstacle.

We don't meet anyone. We climb stairs, and then more stairs, the air warming as we rise. The old-meat stink of the cells is replaced by something worse: a boiling, greasy smell, like bubbling fat. By the time we're aboveground I have a decent guess where we're headed. Red's mother opens a final door and I'm sickened to find out I'm right.

The kitchens are empty. The hearths are banked, the counters bare, the knives hanging clean and wicked from hooks on the wall. And in the corner of the room, huddled in a wire cage like chickens or goats ready for the slaughter, are the children.

They look up when we enter the room, the whites of their eyes gleaming in the dark. Most of them have the glazed, numb expressions of people whose adrenal glands and tear ducts ran dry a long time ago. The last time I saw that look on a kid's face was on my floor of the children's ward, and for a moment I want to split and run, not stopping until I find a world worth lingering in.

One of the kids lifts her chin, body braced against the wire as if she's hoping to get in one last punch before they carve her for the table. I spend half a second admiring the sheer guts of her, and then Red sees her mom.

All the fight runs out of her like cheap dye, leaving her looking like what she is: a frightened girl who wants her mother. Her lips shape a word I don't know and then her mother is on her knees beside the cage, hands jammed through the wire, and her father is smashing his boot against the lock again and again, and if the guards weren't already on their way, they are now.

"Be *quiet*." Eva's strangled whisper arrives long after the ship has sailed. The lock shatters. The children crawl out, some of them still dazed, some of them beginning to cry in sudden, shocking bursts. Red vanishes between her parents, their arms interwoven, their heads bent together. The shape of them—this family trapped in this god-awful horror movie of a world, surrounded on all sides by bad endings, still clinging stubbornly to one another—makes my heart twinge, so I look away.

When I'm done blinking back a weird wave of tears, Red is standing in front of us. She looks from me to Eva and back. "You came after me."

I consider explaining that actually her mom and dad had the whole thing pretty much in hand, but I figure we should get points for effort. "Yep."

Her eyebrows are crimped in the middle. "But you don't even know me."

"Nope."

"Why?" This time, for whatever reason, she addresses the question to Eva.

"Because . . ." Eva flounders, looking around the kitchens as if hoping to find another zombie snake-tarantula to fight rather than finish this sentence. Her eyes skate across mine. She ends quietly, with a wry twist of her lips that isn't half as disdainful as she'd like it to be. "Someone had to."

Red hugs her then, which makes Eva's face do several complicated contortions. It lands on a fixed expression that reminds me of a school calculator that's been asked to perform too many impossible functions and is reduced to flashing ERROR on the screen. She makes eye contact with me over Red's head, a clear plea for help that I pretend not to see.

I always like this part. The happily ever afters that come after are too sweet for me, like grocery store frosting, but this moment right here, when you feel the relief of a bad ending averted, a wrong righted—this is the good shit.

(I give a mental middle finger to Zellandine, because I'm not *running*, I'm being *helpful*, even if Red's parents didn't really need my help.)

Eventually, Red's mother comes to collect her, pausing to give us a dignified nod.

The room empties as the villagers disappear back down the stone steps, led by Red and her family. I watch them go, still full of that heady, giddy pride.

I can tell from Eva's expression—eyes dark, lips slightly parted, head tilted back—that she feels it too. "It's nice, isn't it?" I murmur.

"What is?"

"Being the good guy."

She snorts at me, but her eyes catch mine. I'm smiling brazenly up at her, wondering a little dizzily what it would be like to kiss her for real, on purpose rather than out of necessity, when a voice behind us says cliché-ly, "Well, well, well."

And I know that I have a very few seconds to act. I could run. I could turn and fight. I could prick my finger on the tip of my own knife and hope I fall out of this B-horror movie of a universe. Instead, I do what I've always done when I'm cornered, what I always will do. I text Charm.

In the moment before hands close around my arms and my phone is dashed to the floor, crashing into a dozen useless plastic pieces, and this shitty story takes me in its jaws again, I manage to type nine characters and press send: *atu 709 sos*

7

A CONFESSION: I was totally expecting her to be ugly. Which is pretty fucked up of me, but in my defense, Western folklore persistently and falsely equates a character's physical appearance with their inner morality, so like, it was a pretty safe bet that the evil cannibal queen would look like Anjelica Huston after she peels off her mask in *The Witches*.

But when her goons wrench my arms behind my back and spin me to face her, it turns out she's not ugly at all. She is, in fact, one of the least ugly things I've ever seen (yes, including Prim, who is so beautiful that people squint and blink when they talk to her, like they're trying to have a conversation with the sun). The queen is young and doe-eyed, with long, soft lashes and gently rounded cheeks. Her skin is the phosphorescent white of a Renaissance angel, and her lips are a bright, arterial red, as if she's just eaten a bowl of fresh cherries or, perhaps, the raw hearts of stolen children.

I think, intelligently: *Huh*. And then I think,

slightly more intelligently, my stomach sinking fast: *I know who you are.* "You're—Snow White!" I'm aiming for a nice *j'accuse!* moment, but it's clear from the expressions around me that I'm literally the only person who didn't know.

Snow White smiles at me. It's a very good smile, sweet as springtime, but her voice is pure ice. "You may address me as Your Majesty."

My eyes move of their own accord to Eva. She's putting up a much better fight than me, struggling against three huntsmen as they wrestle her wrists behind her back. One of them knocks the backs of her legs and sends her crashing to her knees. Another buries his fist in her hair and wrenches her face upward, baring the fragile column of her throat. She doesn't look much like a queen compared to Snow White—her face is hard and plain and a little too old, her teeth bared in bitter fury—but looking at her, I feel a big, weird rush of loyalty.

"Sorry," I tell Snow White. "I've already got one of those."

Snow White's sweet smile doesn't falter when she orders her men to strip us of our belongings and lock us up, awaiting punishment for our crimes against queen and country.

So here I am, in the dungeons again. Naturally.

I've seen a decent number of dungeons in the last five years, but these are among the least pleasant. It's the meaty smell of human remains, probably, or maybe the gelatinous burble of the sewers beneath us, or maybe the extreme unlikelihood of our escape. Both our arms are shackled above us and the huntsmen took everything up to, and partially including, our clothes. I'm barefoot and hoodie-less, shivering sporadically in my T-shirt, and Eva's kidney-colored gown is gone. All she's wearing now is one of those shapeless, colorless underdresses that I'm pretty sure is called a *shift*, or maybe a *chemise*, laced up the front with a limp green ribbon. It ought to be at least a little bit sexy, but it just makes her look small and vulnerable, like something recently shelled.

"Okay, so." I cough wetly. "That could have gone better."

Eva's head is tilted back against the wall, her eyes closed. She doesn't respond, so I add a small, insufficient, "Sorry."

She exhales in the manner of someone who is counting slowly to ten before replying. "You're sorry." Her eyes are still closed. "You forced me to accompany you on a mad, doomed mission to rescue a girl I barely know who didn't even need rescuing. You promised me a way out and I risked everything to get it, as I always do—" She pauses, perhaps to count to ten again. "And now I'll die, just like I was always going to. But you—you're *sorry*."

"I mean, I'm also going to die, by the way." Well, probably, depending on how pissed Charm is, and whether she remembers the Aarne-Thompson-Uther index, and whether I can get my hands on the damn mirror again. "So yeah, I'm sorry. But honestly, it feels like you're failing to take responsibility for your own actions here? Like, maybe if you hadn't decided to murder a kid for the crime of being hotter than you, everything would've turned out great. You could've lived to a ripe old age in your own world." I try and fail to keep a green thread of envy out of my voice. I can't imagine the privilege of a long life, but I know I wouldn't waste it with petty, vaguely un-feminist villainy. I'd—

I snap the sentence in half, but the images come anyway, unbidden: Mom's roses blushing in spring, family game night, Charm forcing us all to get matching tattoos on her thirtieth birthday. And—maybe, someday—a place of my own: a houseplant, or even a pet, a daily commute, a savings account because I would have something to save for. A whole life that I'd never have to leave.

I'm breathing in through my nose and out through my mouth,

trying not to cry, when Eva says dismissively, "You don't know what happened."

I lose the pattern of my calm breathing. "You know that red book of fairy tales you found? It belongs to me—belonged, I guess, since you left it behind in your stupid world. My dad gave it to me when I was a kid and I read it at least fifty times and then got a folklore degree and read it fifty more times. I promise, I know how the story goes."

"Of course you do," Eva says to the ceiling. Her voice is mocking, almost smug, as if no one could possibly understand her.

"Hey, I've got nothing but time." I try to spread my arms invitingly and succeed only in rattling my chains. "If you want to give me a long, sympathetic speech about your motivations, be my fucking guest."

Eva answers whip-fast and vicious. "Or maybe you could just *think* for two consecutive seconds. My Snow White was a pretty little girl who sang to songbirds and trusted old women selling apples. I am a witch and a queen who has devoted her life to the accumulation of power. If I'd wanted to kill her, don't you think she would be *dead?*"

I open my mouth, and then close it slowly. Fairy tales are riddled with illogical coincidences and obvious plot holes, but most of us learn to skip over them, like you skip the squeaky step on the staircase. "Okay, I'll play," I say. "Why didn't you kill her?"

Eva is looking at me now, her mouth framed by those bitter lines, her freckles like pinpricks of blood in the dim light. "Because I didn't want to. She was only a child, and I'm not a monster." A defiant lift of her chin. "But I couldn't allow her to stay, either. She was the king's only legitimate heir, and I'd failed to give him any others. After he died, but before she came of age . . . I had power. *Real* power—not whispers behind the throne or politicking in the shadows, like my mother had before me. I alone sat on the throne, I alone wore the crown. I was the *queen*."

It's the kind of line the scheming, power-mad queen might deliver in a fantasy novel, but Eva doesn't look mad. She looks wistful and sad, like a woman recalling the golden days of her youth. "And I knew all of it would vanish the second my stepdaughter married. Or maybe sooner—there were already nasty rumors that I was a witch rather than a woman, that I'd murdered Snow White's father."

"But, like . . ." I run my tongue over my bottom lip, trying to decide if there's a tactful way to ask and resolving that there isn't. "Did you?"

Her shoulders move in what I interpret as a shrug, although it's hard to tell at this angle. "Yes."

"Why?"

Eva's eyes harden. "I already told you. Everything I did, I did to survive." Her lashes shutter. "My husband married me because I was young and he needed heirs. When I failed to give him any, he was . . ." A hideous, weighty pause here. ". . . Displeased."

Oh, Jesus. I'm suddenly sick of these faux-medieval worlds and their shitty gender politics, all the pretty stories we tell about ugly worlds. A terrible sympathy crawls up my throat and lodges there, just behind my tongue. "You've used that word twice now. Failed." I fumble in my grab bag of therapist terminology and emerge with a pathetic "You didn't fail."

Eva has met my insults and jabs with bared teeth, but now, when my voice is low and sincere, she flinches. "What would you know about it?"

I meet her eyes. "Well, for starters, I can't. Get pregnant, I mean." She stares at me for a long time, her eyes wide and suspiciously glassy. I give her my best manacled shrug, because she strikes me as the kind of person who would be forced to kill me if I saw her cry. "Bodies are a real roll of the fucking dice, dude."

She swallows. "They—yes." She swallows again, visibly compartmentalizing, wrenching her story back on the rails. "Anyway. The princes began to arrive before she was fifteen. They lounged around my castle, eating from my table while they wooed my stepchild and plotted to take my throne. She was so young . . . but they came anyway. Every hungry second son who wanted a kingdom of his own."

Eva's eyes are narrowed now, her jaw firm. "So I did what I had to. I chased Snow White away, sent her running into the forest pursued by the only man I was certain would never harm her. Berthold came back with that pig's liver, thinking himself so clever, and I thanked him so prettily."

I recall Berthold's handsome, affable, slightly stupid face. I suppose if I genuinely wanted someone assassinated, he would not be my first choice. It occurs to me that the queen must have known he wouldn't hurt me, either, if I tried to escape.

Eva continues on a long sigh. "I'd hoped never to hear from Snow White again. But she didn't run far enough, and soon there were whispers about a pretty girl hidden in the woods, and the princes were circling like damned vultures, and I thought—if she were dead, or seemed to be dead, they would desist." Another sigh, even longer. "It seems I underestimated their appetites."

Now feels like the moment to apologize or sympathize, or, ideally, to stroke her straggling hair away from her face and press my lips tenderly to her forehead. But we're six feet apart and she probably hates my guts. "Look, Eva—Your Majesty, I—"

"All I wanted was power." Her lips make a bitter shape. "I know how I must sound, what you must think of me, but I only mean power over *myself*. Power to make my own choices, and arrive at my own ends."

"It's called agency." And they said my humanities degree would never come in handy. "It's like, the power you exert over your own narrative."

"It's what protagonists have, then."

"Sometimes even protagonists don't get much of it. I mean, did you read Little Brier-Rose in that book? My story sucks ass."

"Yes, I read it. It does indeed 'suck ass.'" She pronounces the phrase with aristocratic precision, and I make a mental note to teach her more modern swears, provided the two of us survive our forthcoming execution. "But at least it belongs to you. Your name is right there in the title. The only name I have is"—her voice hitches, like a thread catching a stray nail—"the one you gave me."

And, God help me, she sounds genuinely grateful. For a mean little nickname I invented just to annoy her. This strikes me as so backwards and awful that I find myself talking, the words falling out in a guilty, desperate tumble. "Charm—she's my best friend—well, she was, until I screwed it all up—she says the key is narrative resonance."

A flare of hope in Eva's eyes, quickly snuffed. "The key to what?"

I take a short breath. "Moving between worlds."

Eva says nothing, her eyes burning with the same desperate hunger that sent me tumbling into Prim's world in the first place, that keeps me skipping from world to world like a stone across the cold surface of the universe. I find myself looking away, unable to stand the sight of so much hope, even secondhand. "So, the universe is like a book, right? And each world is like a page. And if you tell the same story enough times, you can bleed through to another page."

"You mean—I must write down my own story?" Eva looks like she would open a vein and use her own blood as ink if I told her to.

"No, not literally." Although the thought loosens something in the back of my skull, a question I'd been ignoring. I keep ignoring it. "You have to *enact* a familiar part of your plot. And then you can sort of slip between worlds and go somewhere else." Charm is way better at explaining this stuff than me. I miss her, suddenly and fiercely, the way I haven't let myself in six months and thirteen days. Or, if I'm being honest, five years.

I swallow a knot of snot. "But like, it only works in your *own* story, usually. I'd only ever zapped into other versions of Sleeping Beauty until you and your magic mirror landed me here."

"So . . ." Eva closes her eyes. "We need the mirror."

"I think so, yeah."

"*Why?* It's just a mirror I enchanted to show me the truth."

My chains give an uncomfortable rattle. "I think—well, Zellandine thinks that the universes are getting squooshed together?" I applaud my own use of the passive voice. "So your mirror maybe slipped a little into other stories, and showed you other truths."

I can feel Eva studying me. "It's your fault, isn't it? That's what that fairy meant. The worlds are merging because you won't finish your story."

"Excuse me for not wanting to stand around and wait to die."

"Oh, I quite understand." Her tone turns acidic, blackly triumphant. "But then, I'm the villain."

I don't say anything in my defense, because there's not much to say. Maybe I'm the villain too.

Eventually, I feel Eva's bitterness drain away. "The mirror showed me you, out of all the possible people in all the universes." It sounds almost like an apology. "Why?"

"Well, what were you doing at the time?"

"I was looking into the mirror, obviously." She adds, far less sharply, "Wishing for a way out."

"Well." I remember standing in that hotel bathroom, on the run from another happily ever after that wasn't mine. "So was I. As it happens."

She meets my eyes then, and something passes soft and silent between us. A wordless understanding, a sympathy so profound it approaches symmetry. It makes me think I was wrong, and the mirror in the hotel bathroom showed me my own reflection, after all.

"When you kissed me—" Eva begins, and my heart does a maneuver that feels like jumping off a high dive. "It wasn't desire. You were just trying to trigger this narrative resonance, weren't you?"

My heart belly flops. "Yeah. It didn't work."

"So, without the mirror . . . we're stuck here." Her voice is ashen.

"Looks like it."

Silence unfurls between us. I should be formulating unlikely escape plans, but all I can think about is the sight of Red with her parents, the love strung like a cat's cradle between the three of them. They must have known since the day she was born what fate awaited her, and it didn't stop them caring. It didn't stop my stupid, stubborn parents, either, or my stupid, stubborn best friend. The last time I spoke to her she said we had to talk, and I could tell from her voice that it wasn't about my share of the rent or the laundry I left in the washer until it got moldy. *Sure*, I said, and then I went to my room, pricked my finger, and peaced out without even leaving a note.

And if I die in this sick version of Snow White, I'll never get to tell her how fucking sorry I am.

If Eva hears me crying, she has the decency not to say anything. "I really am sorry," I say thickly. "I'm sorry you didn't get out of your story, but if it helps—at least you're not the villain anymore. If you ever were."

She's quiet so long I don't think she'll answer. And then, when I'm sunk deep in a stupor of regrets and should-haves and aching joints, she whispers, "Thank you."

A few hours after that, they come for us.

I find, if I tilt my shoulders and wrench my arms to the side, that I can just reach Eva's hand as they march us through the castle. Her fingers wrap tight around mine, and we're dragged together toward the climax of our stories.

8

I ALWAYS IMAGINED dying in a hospital room, which is sort of funny because it means some treacherous part of my subconscious always wanted to go back home before the end. I pictured my mom and dad on one side of my bed, Prim and Charm on the other, and lots of really high-caliber drugs singing me to sleep.

I did not picture my bare feet on black stone. I didn't picture an airless courtyard or a low, greasy bonfire. I sure as hell didn't picture anyone walking beside me, her fingers biting into mine as if I am her last hope in the world, or she's mine. My hands are numb and bloodless from hours hanging above my head, but I don't let go.

The huntsmen unshackle our wrists and toss us to the ground before the fire. We crawl toward one another without speaking, our spines bumping as we turn to face the ringed huntsmen. The queen—or Snow White, or whatever twisted amalgamation she is in this world—comes sweeping through their ranks with a supervillain's sense of timing. Her hair is still silky black and her skin is still that unsettling alabaster, but her cheeks seem a little less round this morning, her lips a shade less red.

It feels like a good moment to say something quippy and brave, demonstrating my cocky resilience in the face of certain death, but nothing comes to mind. If I had my phone, I would text Charm in all caps: *NOW'S THE TIME BITCH*

Snow White stops a few feet away from us. "I'm quite cross with you, you know. Children aren't easy to catch." She looks petulant, disturbingly babyish. "They were bound for such a glorious purpose."

"What, dinner?"

Snow White's petulance darkens. "They were meant to keep their queen in the eternal youth that suits her best." Eva makes a small noise of understanding beside me, and Snow White's long-lashed gaze transfers to her. "It was my mother—well, stepmother—who first learned the trick of it." She says it like a secret, although there are huntsmen all around, their ivory necklaces chattering with every tiny movement. "I don't know how old she really was when she married my father, but she looked only a year or two older than me. I think." A doubtful look, as if it's been so long that she can't quite remember. "She might have carried on forever if she hadn't tried to steal the wrong heart." Snow White's fingers tap the white hyphen of her clavicle.

"Look." I wet cracked lips. "That's super awful and traumatizing, and I'm sure you need therapy, but like . . . Why did you turn into the exact same kind of monster? Why couldn't you just chill and live happily ever after?" I'm mostly talking at random, trying to give Charm a few extra seconds to pull off a miracle and rescue me, like she always has before. I wonder if, sometime over the last six months, she stopped sleeping with her ringer on.

Snow White's head tilts, nose scrunching. "It's not really a happily ever after if it *ends*, is it?"

I think I say something here—*it's not like that* or *you don't understand*—but I can't hear it over the rising noise in my head, the sudden bile in my mouth. Is that what I've been doing, these last five years? Trying to outrun my own ending? Throwing away every chance at happiness just because it was fleeting?

I swallow acid. "Every story ends," I whisper. I don't even know which of us I'm trying to convince. Eva shifts beside me so that her shoulder is pressing hard against mine.

Snow White is looking at us like we're very young children; maybe we are, to her. "Well, *yours* will. But I have a few questions before it does." She withdraws something slim and silver from her skirts and turns it to face us. For a confused second I think she's showing us a picture on a phone screen—I see two faces, two sets of desperate eyes—before I understand that I'm looking at a mirror.

My mouth goes dry and sandy. My mind goes perfectly blank. Eva goes very, very still.

Snow White strokes the mirror's surface with one pale fingernail. "This mirror of yours. It has shown me things. Other lands. Other worlds, perhaps." I see the future with helpless, ugly clarity: an immortal cannibal wandering from world to world, plucking princesses from their tales like ripe fruit from the trees. She's warped her own story into a gory horror flick; what could she do to the multiverse?

She asks sweetly, "How do I get there?"

"W-why would you ever want to leave your own world?" Other than the perpetual twilight and freakshow fauna. "You've got a great setup here. A lovely, um, lair, and loyal henchpeople."

Snow White makes a moue. "The villagers are getting restless. They're a tiresome bunch, always *fomenting* and *resisting*. It's harder and harder to get what I need." She pinches the flesh of her throat, where the skin has sagged almost imperceptibly. (I have the unhelpful thought that Dr. Bastille would have an absolute field day with this version of Snow White. "The Fear of Age in the Age of Fear: Representations of the Crone in Modern Folk Horror.")

Snow White smiles her sweet, springtime smile. "They're nothing at all like the little *lambs* I see in other worlds. So I will ask you again: How do I get there?"

I don't answer and neither, somewhat to my surprise, does Eva. Her silence fills me with a weird, reckless pride. "Sorry, I'm just getting the most intense déjà vu, you know? I feel like I was just questioned under torture by an evil queen like, yesterday."

This provokes a brief, whispered argument with Eva ("Torture is a strong word." "Well, if the shoe fits." "If the shoe fits what?" "God, never mind."), at the end of which she clears her throat and says audibly, "I'm sorry I hurt you. I shouldn't have."

It feels like the sort of apology you make because you're pretty sure it's your last chance. I move my hand so that my fingers cover hers, because I'm pretty sure she's right. "It's cool," I say inadequately.

Snow White is watching us closely, looking from our faces to the place where our hands touch. She makes a resigned *tsk*. "I can see you're both terribly stubborn. I'll find my own way. I certainly have the time." She makes an imperious gesture and one of her huntsmen steps forward, drawing his sword with a sound like scraping bone as he comes for us. It's all happening way too fast. I thought I could burn more time bullshitting—I thought Charm would still find her way across the universe for me, even without the mirror, because the rules don't apply to us—

But the huntsman doesn't impale either of us. He steps around us to the edge of the fire and reaches into the coals with the tip of his sword. He extracts an ugly tangle of iron. It looks like the kind of thing you'd see in a museum, a mass of old metal with an obscure, chilling label reading *Scold's bridle, 17th c.* or *Pear of anguish, 18th c.*

Then Eva sobs, harsh and sudden, and I realize that I'm looking at two pairs of iron shoes, the metal straps glowing a dull, hellish red.

I curl my fingers tight around Eva's, but her hand is limp and damp in mine. I turn to face her, kneeling, speaking in a desperate rush. "It's okay, I'm sorry, we're going to be alright." But Eva isn't looking at me, or even at the shoes. Her eyes are on Snow White, who has already forgotten us and is now staring into the mirror's surface with a chilling, predatory patience.

Eva's expression as she looks at the queen is not one of panic, or loathing, or even despair. Her face has an eerie coolness to it, a carved-marble quality that makes my chest hurt for no reason. "Hey, listen, Charm knows we're here. She could still save us, okay?"

Eva's eyes move to mine slowly, squinting as if the two of us are standing on opposite sides of a very wide river.

"I hope she does," she says softly. Then, just as softly, she kisses me.

It's dry and gentle. It feels like an apology, or a farewell. "Thank you." She whispers the words against my lips.

The very small part of my brain that isn't occupied by the imminent approach of my own painful death or the salt-sweetness of her mouth manages to say, "For what?"

"For showing me I do not have to be the villain, the evil step-mother, the Wicked Witch of the East Bro. For giving me . . ." Her eyes move back to Snow White, and her lip curls, revealing a slim white line of bared teeth. "Agency."

It's at this point that Eva begins unlacing the front of her dress. My brain splits into two competing factions, one of which is cheering and sounds a lot like Charm on girls' night at the gay bar, and the other of which is thinking how sad it is that Eva has endured so much, only to lose her mind now. "Eva, babe, what are you doing?"

She doesn't answer, drawing the ribbon slowly out of her shift. Except it's not a ribbon, is it? It's a bodice lace.

A syrupy weight settles over my limbs. I notice small things: the minute tilt of Eva's body away from mine. The taut cord of muscle in her neck, the divot in her cheek as she clenches her jaw, bracing herself to do something terrible and brave and stupid. I reach for her. Too late. Eva has already launched herself across the courtyard, knifing through the air like a falcon with dirty white feathers. She collides with Snow White, and then there's a splintering, shattering sound, like a dropped wineglass. Something sharp slices across my cheek.

The courtyard falls into a numbed silence as every eye looks at the ground, at the place where the magic mirror lies in broken shards. I see our faces reflected in the shards, split and doubled, frozen in shock.

There's a large sliver of glass right beside me, close enough to touch. The face reflected in this piece does not belong to the huntsmen, or either of the queens, or even myself. It's a face framed by a long wing of bleached blond hair, with a septum piercing and an expression suggesting homicidal intent, or at least serious bodily harm. The lips of the face are moving, repeating the same name over and over, interspersed with swears: *Zinnia, Zinnia, goddammit Zinnia.*

"Charm, holy shit—" I reach for the shard and my fingers fall through the glass, into the cold rush of the great nothing between worlds. I feel myself tilting into it, falling forward, but I dig my toes into the stones. "Eva, it's Charm! Come on!"

Eva is crouching before the queen with blood oozing from one nostril. She looks back at me and understanding flashes across her face. But she doesn't run to me. She could have. I want that on the record. She could have taken my hand and run, and left this world under the thumb of its wicked queen for another century or two. She could have chosen to survive, like she always had.

Instead, she draws the bodice lace tight between her hands. It gleams sickly green in the firelight.

Eva nods once to me, with a fey, rueful smile, as if to say, *Well, someone has to,* before she surges to her feet and wraps the ribbon around Snow White's throat.

Warm fingers grab my wrist, pulling hard. The last thing I see before I go is Eva—my not-so-wicked queen, my heroic villain—falling beneath the weight of her enemies.

9

I LAND HARD, flat on my back, feeling like a lump of Play-Doh forced through a cheese grater. The sky above me is no longer low and purple, but a bright, suburban blue crisscrossed by jet trails. A few oak leaves slap peacefully against one another. Damp earth soaks through the back of my T-shirt.

I'm in Charm and Prim's backyard in Madison, a place I wasn't totally sure I'd ever see again and from which I now desperately and ironically want to leave.

"Well, if it isn't Little Miss SOS."

I sit up—a considerable, even noble effort, which Charm does not appear to appreciate in the least. She's kneeling beside me, her nose running badly, her cheeks blotched with ash. Prim is on my other side, her enormous eyes crimped with worry. She brushes dirt from my shoulder, plucks something from the greasy nest of my hair.

Behind them is the tiny metal fire ring they bought for their microscopic yard. There's a pair of flip-flops inside the ring, still smoldering gently, sending up chemical curls of bluish smoke.

I give Charm a quick, woozy smile. "Knew you'd figure it out eventually."

A look of relief crosses her face, there and gone again. She throws a sullen glance at the fire ring. "I liked those shoes."

"Uh." The flip-flops are hot-pink plastic. I can see the dollar store sticker still stuck to the underside of the left shoe. "I owe you a pair?"

Charm shrugs. "It's fine." It's clearly not.

"Okay, whatever. I actually need to go back to where I was, like right now, so if you have another pair to burn that would be great. And maybe a mirror?"

Charm doesn't move. "Aren't you forgetting something?" Her tone is cordial, but her eyes are thin and hard.

"Thank you?"

"Maybe try, 'I'm sorry, Charm.'"

"Okay, I'm *sorry*." It comes out bratty, audibly insincere. "But I really have to—"

"Shut the fuck up and listen for a second?" Charm's civility vanishes; she was never a good bullshitter. Prim winces as Charm leans in. "I agree. Let's recap our situation, shall we? So, first, I tell you I've got something important to talk about, and you say, 'Sure thing, babe!' But then you Spider-Verse into another dimension and leave me hanging." I have the sinking suspicion that this speech has been rehearsed, more than once, with and without slides. Prim is creeping for the back door now, leaving me to my fate. "Second, you don't talk to me for six months. Which is very mature and chill. Then, third, you send me a damn Aarne-Thompson-Uther index number—even though you specifically told me that system was, quote, 'a Eurocentric mess' that 'should be retired from anthropology syllabi'—and failed to respond to any of my requests for clarification. Leaving me to spend the last seven hours frantically acting out the goddamn plot of goddamn Snow White, ever more certain that you'd already bitten into a poison apple or been assaulted by a wandering prince or some—"

There's a lot more to the speech, judging by the rising volume and level of aggression, but all I can think about is Eva's small, sad smile right before she wrapped the bodice lace around Snow White's neck. Like she knew the choice would damn her and didn't care, because at least she was choosing her own damnation.

I interrupt Charm by throwing my arms around her. She stiffens, then hugs me back so hard it feels vindictive. "You're such a little shit, you know that?"

I pull away. "Yeah. And I'm really, really sorry. I *am*. But I have to find a way back into Snow White right now. I have to save—"

Charm tosses both hands in the air. "Some stranger? What about us, Zin? What about *me*, you absolute *turdbucket*."

"I know! I'm sorry, but people need me, okay?"

Charm chews the inside of her cheek before saying, in a voice that could only be accurately measured by the Kelvin scale, "That. Is what I'm trying to tell you. Bonehead."

A small, extremely uncomfortable silence follows this statement, during which Charm watches me with red, tear-sheened eyes and I call myself every bad name I can think of. It strikes me that neither heroes nor dying girls are very good at sticking around, at the ordinary work of living: calling your friends back and remembering their birthdays, going to the doctor for regular checkups, taking care of the people you love.

Charm sits back, cross-legged, ripping disgustedly at the grass.

"You're so busy mucking around in other worlds you don't even care about the freaky shit happening in your own."

"Like what kind of freaky shit?" I ask, very mildly. But I think I know.

"Like fairy tale shit. I bought one of those frozen apple pies—shut up, they're good—and when we cut into it we found a bunch of blackbirds. Prim's shoes turned to glass one night while she was dancing. Your mom's roses went nuts in December, blooming while there was still snow on the ground."

I unglue my tongue from the roof of my mouth and say carefully, "That's not so bad, is it?"

"Well, it's not great." Charm is tearing the grass up in great handfuls now, her nail beds stained neon. "The birds were all dead and putrefied. Prim's shoes shattered under her—*nine* stitches, she missed weeks of class. And your mom's roses died down to the roots. She tore them all up."

"Oh."

Charm fixes me with a blunt blue eye. "Is it your fault?"

"Maybe."

"Will it get worse?"

"Uh, maybe. Yeah." I look away from her. "If I don't stop."

"Then . . ." Charm presses the heels of her hands into her eyes. "Jesus, why don't you?"

"I should. I will! But . . ." But somewhere along the line, Eva became one of the people I'm supposed to take care of, and she needs me, and the physical laws of the multiverse can go straight to hell. "But first I need to borrow your phone."

Charm stands. She stares down at me with an expression somehow worse than anger, or even disappointment. It's a sort of bitter, self-directed chagrin, as if she's annoyed that she allowed herself to be disappointed by me again. She slams her phone down on the plastic card table as she leaves.

It takes me a minute to guess her passcode (8008, because Charm still has a seventh grader's sense of humor), and another minute to find the faculty contact information on Ohio University's site.

The phone slips against the clammy sweat of my face. "Hi, this is Zinnia Gray. Is Dr. Bastille available?"

❁ ❁ ❁

"So—AGAIN, HYPOTHETICALLY—HOW COULD the protagonist get back into that Snow White story without the magic mirror?"

Dr. Bastille sighs on the other end of the line. It seems to go on a very long time, as if she's holding her phone in front of a box fan. "Well, *hypothetically*, if you were my student and you came into my office and told me . . . everything you just told me"—over the last six to eight minutes, I've given her the SparkNotes version of my life, framing it all somewhat unconvincingly as the plot of a very meta novella I'm working on—"I would be legally and morally obligated to refer you to campus counseling services."

"Good thing I'm not your student anymore, huh."

"Zinnia, that's not better. You see how that's not better, right? If a random person came into my office to talk about the fairy tale multiverse, I would probably swallow my personal convictions about law enforcement's role in the violent maintenance of race and class hierarchies"—this is ivory tower speak for *fuck the cops*—"and call security."

"Sure, I get that, but what if I was very convincing and desperate-seeming, and you were sort of compelled to advise me despite your better judgment?" I'm trying to bully her into a specific narrative role—the expert consultant/holder of arcane knowledge who offers wise counsel to the protagonist in their hour of need and saves their bacon—but I can feel Dr. Bastille resisting it. She's never much liked playing prescribed roles.

I hear her pulling the phone away from her face, saying *I'll just be a minute, love* to someone else. A woman's voice says something about dinner reservations in a tone suggesting they have been made and broken before.

Dr. Bastille sighs into the receiver again. "Alright. Given the parameters of the story you just told me, it is my professional opinion that you've written yourself into a corner."

"What does that mean?"

"It means you're screwed."

"I—okay." The grass feels very cold on my bare feet, the sky very high above me.

"You said the only way to cross into other tale types was by way of a particular enchanted object. A useful MacGuffin which is now, according to you, broken. So your protagonist doesn't have a magic mirror, and neither does the villain-slash-love-interest—a trend in popular fiction which I find beneath you, by the way"—Dr. Bastille elects to ignore my sighed *I wish*—"and I don't think the physical laws of this universe allow for the creation of enchanted objects. Do they?"

I'm circling the fire pit now, letting the plastic-smelling smoke sear my eyes. "I guess not."

"Which seems like it might be a good thing, because your protagonist's hypothetical wanderings were doing substantial damage to the fabric of the space-time continuum, were they not?"

"But like, why?" My voice goes high on the last word, wobbling perilously. "Why is it such a big deal if I—I mean, my character—doesn't just lie down and wait for the trolley to hit her? Why can't she run away?"

I can hear a familiar creaking through the line, as if Dr. Bastille is leaning back in her office chair and pinching the bridge of her nose. She did this often in our advisee meetings. "In this novella, you've posited narratives as literal worlds. So stories are the organizing principle of the multiverse—which raises some serious world-building questions, by the way, like where these story-verses come from in the first place, since the existence of any story implies the existence of a storyteller." She pauses to address her date: *No, you go ahead, I'll meet you there.* "Anyway, you've created a universe that runs on plot, and a main character who smashes plots like a human wrecking ball. In refusing to complete her narrative arc, she is compromising the integrity of the universe."

"Oh." The smoke scorches my eyes, burns the inside of my nose. "Then this is it. It's over."

"It does seem a dissatisfying climax."

"Yeah. Well." My nose is running badly now. "Thanks for your time."

"Sure." The creak of her chair, the shush of arms sliding into coat sleeves. Dr. Bastille's voice softens very slightly when she says, "I'd be happy to read it, when it's done."

"Read what?"

"The . . . never mind. Good luck, Zinnia." She hangs up.

I set Charm's phone back on the card table and sink slowly to my knees. My eyes are too full of tears to see much beyond fractal green, but I search the grass with my hands, crawling in circles. All I find are beer caps, a few waterlogged roaches, the sharp tops of acorns.

There are no shards of magic mirror in Charm's backyard. Which means Dr. Bastille was right. I'm screwed, and so is Eva.

* * *

I PACE THE yard for a while, inventing and dismissing a dozen unlikely schemes. It occurs to me eventually that I'm doing what my therapist would call *bargaining,* and that bargaining is a stage of grief.

Charm and Prim are in the kitchen, speaking in tense, low voices. They stop when the screen door shuts behind me. Charm gives me a searching stare, which I return blankly until she turns back to the dishes. Prim looks fretfully between the two of us for a moment, but there's no real question which side she'll pick. She unfolds a dish towel and dries a mixing bowl at Charm's side.

I walk down the hall to the bedroom that is supposedly mine but which actually functions as a walk-in closet. I pick my way through yoga mats and wrapping paper, trash bags of winter clothes, a laundry basket filled with velvet gowns, pewter goblets, all the crap I hadn't sold at the Ren faire before I disappeared. The futon is buried, so I sit on a box of unassembled furniture with THREE IN ONE! written across the side in bubbly, childish letters.

I stare at the wall and test the words on my tongue: *The end.* It's not such a bad ending, I guess. It's a sort of cosmic compromise with the universe. I don't get to magically cure my disease and con my way out of my own plot, but at least I didn't drop dead at twenty-one; Eva doesn't get to live as a hero, but at least she didn't die a villain.

It's not exactly happily ever after, but that's a pretty bullshit concept anyway. Honestly, I don't even know why I'm crying.

Later, long after the clink of dishes has faded and the tears have left my cheeks stiff and dry, the door inches open. I assume it's Charm coming back for round two, but it's Prim. She steps easily through the detritus and clears a space on the futon. Neither of us say anything for a while. She just sits there with her perfect posture and her perfect hair, and I notice the fine lines at the corners of her mouth, the slight pucker of skin beneath her eyes.

She doesn't look old or anything, just ordinary. Like any other girl who wakes up every morning and makes coffee a little stronger than she prefers because that's how her wife likes it, who shops at the farmer's market every Saturday, who will look in the mirror in ten years and start googling eye creams even though her wife insists she's always had a thing for crow's feet. Maybe happily ever after isn't a totally bullshit concept, after all; maybe, if I can't have my own, I can at least find the decency not to ruin this one.

I inhale. "I know I've been a shitty friend. And a lackwit, and all those other things Charm called me."

"Well, actually." Prim gives a small, embarrassed cough. "I sent that text."

I don't say anything, relishing the rare feeling of having the moral high ground. Prim squirms for a minute before adding, in a rush, "I was upset because Charm was hurt—*again*—and she was just going to keep giving you chances to hurt her, and I didn't want to watch."

Okay, maybe I'm not on the high ground after all. "I know. It's just . . . I guess I wasn't ready to talk about appointments and treatment plans and all that stuff. I didn't want to be *worried* over, you know? I wanted to make my own choices, choose my own consequences, live my own—"

"Zinnia," Prim interrupts, softly and gravely. Her gaze is very sober. "We want to adopt."

"Um, that's good? Does this place allow pets?"

She blinks at me, and an expression of great pity crosses her face.

"No. It doesn't." Her eyes move to the box of furniture I'm sitting on. I look down and notice for the first time that there is a picture of a blissful-looking baby on the front. The small print explains that the contents of the box can be used as a bassinet, crib, and toddler bed as your "little one" grows.

I feel suddenly very, very young and very, very stupid. "Oh," I say weakly.

"That start-up offered Charm a full-time position last year, and she took it. So the timing feels right, and it turns out I want children very much, once I realized they could be obtained outside of heteronormative and patriarchal conceptions of marriage." I remember Charm telling me last year that Prim signed up to audit some classes at UW; apparently she liked them.

"Wow, I'm so . . ." Happy? Terrified? Abruptly conscious of the passage of time and fearful of my changing position in what was, until recently, a trio of friends? My voice shrinks. "I didn't know."

"Well, you wouldn't." Prim doesn't sound especially sympathetic. "You left when Charm tried to tell you. She wanted to ask about using this bedroom, once the paperwork was filed."

"Oh," I say again, even more weakly. I dampen my lips. "So . . . how's it going? I heard it can take a while."

Prim's cool composure slips. She looks away and swallows twice. "We never filed the paperwork, actually. Charm hasn't signed it."

A chill settles in the pit of my stomach, a premonition of guilt. "Why not?"

Prim's posture is imperfect now, her shoulders bent. "She says it's because she's not ready to give up beer, but I think she's scared."

"Of what?"

Prim rarely snaps—you can take the princess out of the royal court, but you can't take the royal court out of the princess, or something—but now she snaps, "Of doing it without her best friend, maybe."

The guilt arrives, cold and heavy as a swallowed stone. "Look, I'm really, *really*—"

She interrupts. "Or maybe she's just scared of messing it up, the way her parents did. Adoption . . . wasn't easy for her." This is a massive understatement; I once overheard her mom lamenting Charm's (unremarkable, classically teenaged) behavior to my mom. *You'd just think she'd be more grateful, wouldn't you?* Mom had looked at her like she was a new kind of fungus on one of her rose bushes. I'd never told Charm, but it's not like she didn't know the score.

"Yeah, I can see that."

Prim picks at invisible lint on the futon. "I'm scared, too, to tell the truth. My childhood was not particularly easy either, but . . ." She shrugs, as if the next thing she says isn't that important. "I wish I could talk to my mother."

I move over to the futon, sitting so close our shoulders touch. "Hey, at least there's no wicked fairies in this world." It's an effortful joke.

Prim laughs, equally effortfully. "Well, not yet. But I saw those glass slippers, and the dead birds. This world is not so safe as I had hoped."

The guilt doubles, or maybe quadruples. It's a wonder I have any room left for ordinary human organs. I fumble for something comforting to say and emerge with "No world is very safe, in my experience."

It seems, inexplicably, to help. Prim straightens again and nods at no one in particular. "No. Which means all that matters really is who you have standing at your side. Charm and I have each other, and if that has to be enough, it will." She pauses, perhaps having run out of grand proclamations. "But where I come from, fairy godmothers are traditional. Twelve seems excessive, but if I had a daughter I should hope for at least one."

She meets my eyes as she says the word *one*, her expression simultaneously arch and a little anxious. Like she's just asked me to carry something large but fragile, infinitely precious, and isn't sure I'm up to the task. Like she wants to trust me, but isn't sure she should.

I have the absurd urge to kneel. Fresh tears prickle in the corners of my eyes. "That would be—*I* would be—" I swallow. "Like, I know I haven't been that reliable lately, and I can't promise that my GRM will stay in remission or whatever—but it would be my honor."

Prim nods without breaking eye contact. Her gaze feels like a sword touching each of my shoulders, not especially gently. "Good." She inhales sharply and draws something from her pocket. "We'll talk more when you come back, then."

I know I'm not at my sharpest—having been zapped into a dozen different universes, lightly tortured, imprisoned, kissed, nearly executed, rescued, and chastised by pretty much everyone I've ever met—but this feels like a real left turn in the conversation. "Come back from where?"

Prim hands me the thing she took out of her pocket. It's long and silver, and in its surface I catch the blue flash of her eyes, the glare of the cheap light fixture above us.

It's a long, broken shard of mirror. "I pulled it from your hair when you first arrived."

I could kiss her. I could ask her what the hell took her so long. I could weep, because hope is so much more terrifying than despair.

I draw a breath that shakes only slightly. "Tell Charm I'm coming back, okay? For good, this time. Cross my heart." I don't wait for Prim to agree, or tell me to be careful. I hold the shard so that it reflects a jagged piece of my own face, and whisper to it: *Mirror, mirror.*

10

IN AN OBJECTIVE and literal sense, there's no way Eva is the fairest of them all—her face is too square and her mouth is too wide, and she's maybe a smidge too old—but that's the face the mirror shows me when I ask, and the mirror never lies. Maybe beauty really is in the eye of the beholder, and if the beholder is willing to ditch her friends and damage the fabric of space and time for someone, the mirror logically assumes they're past the point of objective beauty standards.

Which I guess I am, because Eva's face makes it suddenly difficult to breathe. I fall toward her, diving through nowhere, feeling like a smear of toothpaste being squeezed out of some cosmic tube. I'm braced to land in hellish chaos—a burning castle filled with murderous huntsmen, perhaps, or a public execution—but I find myself standing in a small, white-washed room with lots of windows and no blood at all.

It doesn't look like the sort of room that could

conceivably exist anywhere in Evil Snow White's castle, or even in the same world. The light slanting through the windows is an ordinary dusky gold rather than the malevolent violet of endless twilight; the fire in the hearth is cheery and warm and probably was not made to heat iron shoes or boil human soup. The whole place reminds me strongly of Zellandine's hut, except a little emptier and newer.

I would assume I'd made a wrong turn in nowheresville if it weren't for Eva. The queen—*my* queen—is sitting at a small table, fiddling with something shiny.

I make a small, embarrassing sound in the back of my throat, nearly a whimper; she looks up.

And she's—fine. A little tired, maybe, but not tormented or terrified. There's a crust of red around one nostril, but no mortal wounds. She's still wearing her sheer white shift, grimed with prison filth, but there's a plain cloak draped over her shoulders now. Her feet are bare on the floor, the skin smooth and unhurt.

One side of her mouth tilts. There's a light in her eyes that doesn't quite manage to be a wicked gleam. "Why, Lady Zinnia," she drawls. "Have you come to rescue me?"

"I . . ." I glance around the room, which persists in being almost aggressively nonthreatening. "This was a whole lot cooler in my head. How come you don't need rescuing?" I remember, very distantly, wishing more of the princesses would rescue themselves. "The last thing I saw was the huntsmen coming for you, on account of how you assassinated their immortal monarch."

"Yes, well, you left before it got interesting."

She says it with a sly bat of her eyelashes, but another pound of guilt settles in my stomach. I'm surprised there's room, at this point. "I didn't mean to." I make myself meet her eyes. "Leave, I mean."

Eva shrugs, performatively careless. "Why not? I would have."

"But like, you didn't. You could have, but you chose to stay." Which means an actual storybook villain has more moral fiber than I do, apparently. "Anyway, Charm pulled me through the mirror. I wouldn't have left you there, I swear."

Eva looks away and says quietly, "I know." She looks back. "Maybe that's why I stayed." The intensity of the eye contact following this statement makes me think she doesn't hate my guts at all, actually, and if the multiverse stopped breaking and people stopped attacking us for a minute we could do a lot better than a couple of hurried, clumsy kisses.

"Here, sit down." Eva gestures to a second chair. She isn't blushing, but her throat is pinker than I remember it being. "If you'd stayed another thirty seconds or so, you would have seen Red and her people storm the courtyard, cast Snow White's crown into the fire, and declare the glorious revolution."

I blink a few times. I'm not sure any version of Snow White ends with an anti-royalist uprising. "No shit?"

"None whatsoever. Apparently, her parents were highly placed in the revolutionary movement, and Red convinced them to accelerate their plans on our behalf." Eva's smile is small and wry. "It never occurred to me that the person you save might save you in turn. Perhaps survival is less solitary than I'd thought."

I think of Charm and Prim, who saved me, who are still hoping I'll stick around and hold up my half of the bargain. "That's been my experience, yeah." My voice sounds thick in my ears.

"I believe they'll crown Red as their new queen soon. I mean, I overheard some very dense discussion of the monarchy as a symbolic rather than political position, and something about a body of elected representatives, which all sounds rather messy, but"—Eva shrugs—"I suppose it's close enough. The innocent girl sits upon her throne, the wicked witch is dead."

"Is she? Dead, I mean."

Eva looks at my face and then quickly away. "No," she says softly. "I don't know how her story will end, or whether redemption is possible for a creature like that, but I . . . asked that she be spared. They will build a glass tomb for her so that anyone who likes can see the proof of her defeat. And make sure she still sleeps."

I have an urge to reach across the table and put my hand over hers, which I squelch before remembering that I'm not a dying girl or a hero anymore. I put my hand over hers. "So how did you end up here? Wherever here is."

Eva's hand turns palm-up under mine. Her neck is now a definite shade of coral. "I didn't feel I should linger long in the castle. Red and her parents seemed grateful, but their friends didn't seem especially fond of witches or queens, so I left. And I found a little house waiting for me in the woods, just like there always is." Her smile this time looks like hard work. "So I suppose I shall rot away in a little hut, after all. It's better than being tortured to death."

I can hear the compromise in her voice, the same mediocre deal I cut in my own world. She's not dead, but she's still nameless and power-less, still trapped at the margins of a story that doesn't belong to her. Not a happy ending, but then, she's not the main character.

I find myself grasping desperately for alternatives. A voice that sounds very much like my therapist says, *Bargaining again?* I ignore it. "What if—maybe you could . . ." My eyes fall to the table, where she's arranged a glittering jigsaw of mirror shards. She's fit them all carefully back into the battered silver frame, with a single gap left for a missing piece. "You could come back to my world. With me. The mirror still works—"

Eva's fingers tighten around mine, but her voice is wistful. "And who would I be in your world?"

"I don't know, nobody in particular I guess?"

"Here I'd hoped to be somebody, one day. Isn't that silly?"

I want to shake her. "I didn't mean literally nobody, just like, not magical or royal or whatever. You could be a chemist or a fortune-teller or something, anything you wanted. I'd help."

She sighs in a way that reminds me forcibly of Dr. Bastille. "I know. Thank you." She slides her hand gently away from mine. "But I heard what Zellandine told you. I can't go with you, and you can't stay here without causing great harm." Her voice lowers. "We can't keep running from our stories forever."

"No." I don't know whether I'm agreeing or disagreeing with her. My lips feel numb.

Eva rises slowly from the table and takes a book from the shelf. The cover is worn red cloth, with a purplish stain on the back. "This was here when I arrived, somehow. It belongs back in your world, I suppose." She tries to say it casually, but I see the way her thumb moves along the spine.

I reach for the book with a feeling of profound unreality, flipping through the pages because that's what you do when someone hands you a book and you don't know what to say. Rackham's art flutters past like tangled shadows: branches and ball gowns, towers and thorns, dozens of dark tales told so many times they came true.

I think of Dr. Bastille saying tartly, *The existence of any story implies the existence of a storyteller.* I guess there must have been a first time each of these stories was told, somewhere in the way-back reaches of time, centuries before the Grimms ever tried to turn a profit on them. It was probably just some ordinary person whispering across a fire or carving pictures into whalebones or daubing mud on the walls of a cave, casually calling a new universe into existence.

It occurs to me with a sudden, slightly hysterical surge of hope that

I am a pretty ordinary person, myself. That the only thing stopping me from writing a new story is the fact that I'm bad at it, and dropped my creative writing class after three weeks rather than suffer a B+. I felt self-conscious and stupid every time I sat down to write, very aware that I was just making things up. But maybe every story is a lie until it isn't; maybe I'm not the one who has to tell it, anyway.

"Do you have a pen?" My voice sounds completely normal, as if my pulse is not double-timing in my throat, as if my whole heart isn't resting on the success or failure of this extremely sketchy plan.

Eva produces a trimmed feather and a pot of ink, looking at me as if faintly worried about mental stability. I turn to the very back of the book, past the afterword and the publisher's note about the typeface, past Rackham's final, curling vine. There are three extra pages at the end, entirely blank.

I set the quill to the page and write: *Once upon a time . . .*

And I swear, the universe listens. I feel it as a silent thrumming through the soles of my feet, the plucking of a string too vast to hear. The windows rattle in their frames.

I add another clumsy sentence or two about a princess who grew into a queen who became a villain and then, eventually, a hero. I spin the book to face Eva and slide it across the table. "Your turn."

She reads the page and her face goes tight and still. A muscle moves in her jaw. "I don't know what happens next."

I twirl the feather. "It's your story. You tell me."

I can't tell if she understands what I'm trying to do, or if she thinks the whole thing is some sort of inane therapy exercise, but when she takes the pen, her hand is shaking. She sits for a while, rolling the quill in her fingertips and staring at the page with a faint frown, before she begins to write.

It takes a lot longer than I expect it to. Eva pauses after every sentence to do some more staring and frowning. She blots out entire paragraphs and starts them over, often several times in a row. At one point she actually makes a motion as if she's going to ball the page up and toss it away like a novelist in a bad movie, before apparently recalling that she's writing in my favorite childhood book. She restrains herself to crossing out another paragraph.

I watch her, listening to the sound I can't really hear, hoping for a future that doesn't yet exist.

Night has fallen by the time she finishes. She doesn't set her pen down in triumph or anything, but I know the story is done because I feel it. The thrumming stops. The air changes. It's like someone has opened an invisible door and let in a breeze that smells like frost and fresh apples.

Eva gives a little sigh and un-hunches herself from the page.

"Looks good," I say over her shoulder, and the queen startles so badly she chokes. Apparently she hadn't noticed me getting up, rummaging for candles, asking three or four times if she was hungry, and eventually giving up and standing behind her. I thump her good and hard on the back. "Needs a title, though."

When Eva stops coughing, she flips back to the beginning of her story and runs her finger across the empty space above the words *once upon a time*. "I don't know what to call it." Her voice is hoarse and low. "I've never done this before."

I drag my chair around the table so I can sit catty-corner to her. "Well, it's your call, but the Grimms generally named their stories after the protagonist."

She goes still beside me. Only her eyes move, meeting mine. I assure myself that it's just the candles that make them look that way, bright and burning. Nobody's eyes are full of literal light; nobody's gaze actually smolders.

She writes a name without speaking.

I read the word, pretending not to notice the pair of watery tear drops blotting the page beside it. "You know I was just teasing when I called you that. You can choose any name you want."

"I have." Her tone might manage to be imperious, if there weren't tears in it. "How do we know if it . . . worked?"

I don't answer. I slide the last shard of mirror across the table, the one Prim plucked from my hair, and fit it neatly into the frame. Our faces look up at us from the surface, fissured and cracked, but exactly as we are: a skinny, sharp-chinned woman in a dirty T-shirt and a hard, hungry queen with a surprising number of freckles.

The only difference is what's behind us. There are no whitewashed walls in the mirror. It's distant and blurred, but I think I see a rich, rolling landscape, a stone shape that might be a castle. A new story, unfolding around us in all directions.

I take Eva's hand and place it gently on the mirror's surface. Her fingers fall through the glass as if it's an open window.

She doesn't drag me into the space between worlds this time. She looks at me with a question in her eyes, and I shrug. "One more time can't hurt, can it?"

Eva smiles. We fall together into the vast nowhere, where my imaginary body fights for air that doesn't exist, where the only real thing is the heat of her hand holding tight to mine.

11

This is, depending on how you count it, either my forty-ninth or fiftieth happily ever after, but I don't mind. It turns out I'm not quite sick of them yet.

It shouldn't be daylight for hours, but somehow we've arrived at that perfect moment just after dawn, when the air rushes away from the horizon and lays tall grasses low. The sunlight transforms the frost into dew and the dew into mist, which coils catlike around our skirts. There are trees surrounding us again, but they aren't dark or tangled. They stand in long, neat lines, their branches spreading low. An orchard, at dawn.

Eva is turning in a slow, wary circle, as if she's waiting for someone to leap out from behind a tree and shout, "Seize her!" No one does. Instead, the mist parts to reveal a pale stone castle standing on a distant hill. It's not very big or grand—in castle terms, it might even be called modest—and there's a shabbiness to it that suggests empty halls and unclaimed thrones. But it's enough for Eva, I can tell. Her mouth falls open as she looks at it.

A throne of one's own. A happily ever after fit for a queen. I have to remind myself forcefully that I'm not a queen or even a princess, and this story doesn't belong to me.

I expect Eva to stride straight for the castle, but she turns back to me. Her smile is wide and young, almost giddy. There are no convenient candles to blame for the bright blaze of her eyes. "It's better than I imagined."

I grab my own elbows so I don't do anything stupid, like fling myself at her. "Yeah, it's not bad." It takes a moment to unglue my tongue from the roof of my mouth. "It suits you."

A little wariness creeps back across her face. Her tone turns haughty, the way it does when she's uncertain. "Do you think it might suit you, as well?"

"I mean, sure." I find it easier to speak to her if I close my eyes. "But you know I can't stay."

"Because of the harm it would do to the universe." There's a flattering amount of grief in her voice.

"Yeah, and because Charm would murder me." And Prim would hide the body, and my parents would testify in court that I deserved it. "There are these people, back in my world, who need me."

"Still playing the hero." A note of bitterness this time.

"No, I need them too. It's just—they're my story. And I can't keep running away from them." I scrape together enough guts to open my eyes and find Eva looking at me with whatever the opposite of pity is—admiration, maybe, or compassion. I dig my fingertips into my elbows.

"So anyway. Enjoy your happily ever after."

Her lips curve in an expression too sad to be called a smile. "You know, I don't think I believe in those."

I raise my eyebrows at the bucolic perfection surrounding us, a Cézanne painting come to life. "Could've fooled me."

Eva takes a step nearer and hands me the red-bound book of fairy tales. "The last line was the hardest to get right. I tried to write it in the usual way, but it gave me goosebumps. It felt like a promise that couldn't be kept, a story that couldn't end."

I flip to the last page of my book, no longer blank. Her hand must have stopped shaking by then, because the last three words are firm and smooth on the page: *She lived happily*. The period is an emphatic black circle.

And then I'm on the sudden, embarrassing verge of tears. Maybe because I've gone a really long time without eating or sleeping and my nerves are shot. Maybe because I've fallen pretty hard for the (former) villain and don't want to leave her. Maybe because it never occurred to me that it could be enough just to *live*, as happily as you can, for as long as you have.

There are more wet splotches on the page now, distorting Eva's neat handwriting. She's gracious enough not to mention it.

I hear the soft tread of her bare feet, then the rustle of leaves, like she's plucked something from a branch. When she returns, she stands close enough that I can see the hem of her shift, the grass-stained ends of her toes. If I had the nerve to look up, her face would be inches away from mine. I don't look up.

"So. I will stay, and you will go home, and both of us will live happily." Eva's voice is light and easy. I nod at my book and cry a little harder.

She reaches for my hand and turns it palm up. She places something smooth and round in it: an apple. The skin is a glassy, poisonous red that only exists in fairy tales.

My laugh is watery. "Old habits, huh?" I scrub my face on my own shoulder. "Will I fall into an endless sleeping death if I take a bite?"

Eva's breath stirs my hair. "If you did, I know someone who would kiss you back to life."

On this, both our stories agree: a girl in an accursed sleep is woken by her true love. It's a strange point of plot convergence, a resonance that makes my skin prickle. I elect to ignore it; it feels too much like hope.

Instead, I look up at Eva and raise the apple to my lips. She watches my teeth pop through the skin and her eyes go suddenly wide and dark, as if she's just solved some very complex equation.

I'd like to say something seductive and clever, which maybe raises the chances of this scene ending with us making out, but what I say is, "You know there's no kiss in the Grimms' version, right? Snow White just barfs up a chunk of apple."

A cool finger touches my chin, tilts my head upward until I'm looking straight into the black satin of Eva's eyes. "This is my story, and I'll tell it how I like." If we were in a sexier sort of romance, I might call the tone of her voice a *purr*; I might note that her finger is still curled beneath my chin, that if I stood on my tiptoes our lips would touch.

"Uh." I swallow. The apple is sharp in my throat. "I don't actually have to leave right this second. I mean, I told Prim I'd come back, and I meant it, but I didn't give her like, a specific date and time—"

I don't finish the sentence, because the queen kisses me, and I kiss her back. I don't even have to stand on tiptoes, because she bends to meet me.

It's technically our third kiss, I guess, but the first two barely count. They were conducted under stressful conditions and interrupted by trips through the multiverse or attempts on our lives. Nothing interrupts us this time. We stand at the crossroads of our stories, in a kingdom of two, kissing in the rising light of a new world. We do a lot more than kiss, actually, but that's between the queen and me.

Later—like, *much* later, not that I'm bragging—we leave the orchard and wander over the hills, into the castle. We drift through the halls without speaking, our hands clasped, our steps unhurried. But eventually I find a staircase that circles upward, and a round room waiting at the top of the tallest tower.

Eva kisses me once more, a brief heat against my cheek. "Thank you," she whispers, and slips something round and smooth into my left hand.

"We have apples in Ohio, you know."

"Good," she says. "Then you can save this one for the very end." She says it lightly, but I can see that vast equation in her eyes again. I guess evil queens can't help but scheme.

Eva holds her magic mirror to face me. I just stand there for a minute, looking at her, trying hard to convince myself that this is enough, that I'm content. My reflection in the mirror doesn't buy it; my face is pale and sharp, fractured with grief.

At least this time, when I touch the mirror and fall into the space between worlds, I'm not running away or rushing to anyone's rescue. I'm not looking for a new once upon a time or hoping, secretly and shamefully, for my happily ever after. This time I'm just trying to live. Happily.

❀ ❀ ❀

I OPEN MY eyes when my feet touch cold tile. I'm standing in Charm and Prim's tiny bathroom, looking at my own face in their medicine cabinet mirror. I can hear small, domestic sounds through the door: the hum of a vacuum, the clink of a spoon.

I can't make myself open the door just yet, so I study the apple in my hand. It's that same slick, unlikely red, but this one isn't unblemished. It looks like someone has pushed their fingernail through the skin, again and again, writing a message into the white flesh:

BITE ME

I smile, a little painfully, and then Eva's voice echoes in my skull: *I know someone who would kiss you back to life*, and *for the very end*. I stop smiling. My heartbeat sounds uneven, very far away. I wonder, distantly, why I'm so surprised. When you save someone, sometimes they save you right back.

I don't know if it would actually work. I don't know if Eva would wait for me that long, or if her kiss could cure me, or if we would irrevocably break the rules of the universe. But what rules would we be breaking, really? An unlucky girl falls into a terrible sleep; her true love wakes her. That piece of the plot could belong to either of us, couldn't it? It feels like a loophole, a cheat code, a chance. It feels like hope.

My story will still end—every story does—but I no longer know when, or how, or where. All I know for sure is what happens next, and I find it's enough for me.

I set the apple carefully on the edge of the sink and clear my throat. "Hey, uh, guys?"

The vacuum goes silent. A muffled conversation follows ("Who the fuck was that?" "It sounded like—" "I will *flay* her.").

I raise my voice, smiling at my own face in the mirror. "I'm home."

ACKNOWLEDGMENTS

I wasted half a day trying to come up with a tortured Snow White parallel for these acknowledgments (Perhaps my publishing team could be compared to seven life-saving dwarves? Could I do anything with the magic mirror bit?) but I failed hard, so all I have to offer is this humble list and a lot of gratitude. This story owes its life to:

My agent, Kate McKean, who simply does not quit.

My editors, Jonathan Strahan and Carl Engle-Laird, who trust me and doubt me to precisely the right degrees.

My cover artist, David Curtis, and the entire team at Tordotcom, who did not have to go this hard, but who did anyway. Special thanks to Irene Gallo, Greg Collins, Christine Foltzer, Matt Rusin, Oliver Dougherty, Isa Caban, Giselle Gonzalez, Megan Barnard, Eileen Lawrence, Amanda Melfi, Dakota Griffin, Jim Kapp, Sarah Reidy, Lauren Hougen, Rebecca Naimon, Michelle Li, Kyle Avery, and everyone from Tor Ad/Promo.

The expertise of J. D. Myall, who saved me from myself, and the thoughtful, patient, generous insight of E. J. Beaton, H. G. Parry, Shannon Chakraborty, Rowenna Miller, and the rest of the blessed bunker.

The friends who've seen us through the first years of this frankly miserable decade, who have made us brunch and babysat the kids and left Gatorade on the front porch when we were sick.

My brothers, Eli and Larkin, who provided the memes and movie nights.

My kids, who provide the chaos, and Nick, who provides the order—and the humor and the food and the music, who is the very marrow of my life, the heat at the center of everything, and who is—as I type this—cajoling a three-year-old out of the kitchen cabinet.